MAIN FORCE ...

The impact of the first of two of the cannon shells exploding against his shin-bone and the second within his chest cavity propelled the shattered corpse of the rear gunner out of his safety belt and halfway through the metal doors of the rear entry port as a third shell ignited a flare. In a matter of seconds, the Frazer Nash turret was reduced to a chaos of flaring oxygen lines and exploding ammunition.

The Nightfighter's second salvo riddled the port wing-tanks, and a ricochet, having removed the co-pilot's index finger at the knuckle, also severed the port fuel lead just below the master engine cock, and the electrical fuel pumps continued to pour 100 octane petrol onto the cockpit floor at the rate of a gallon every twenty seconds.

By then the port wing-tanks were already alight, ignited by a blow-back of flame from the inner exhaust damper. Seconds later the petrol vapour trapped in the nose of the Stirling exploded with a roar and detonated the bomb load as the sergeant pilot still pressed the control column forward in a futile, instinctive dive ...

Guy Kingston

Main Force

MAYFLOWER
GRANADA PUBLISHING
London Toronto Sydney New York

Published by Granada Publishing Limited
in Mayflower Books 1978

ISBN 0 583 12827 0

A Mayflower Original

Granada Publishing Limited
Frogmore, St Albans, Herts, AL2 2NF
and
3 Upper James Street, London W1R 4BP
1221 Avenue of the Americas, New York, NY 10020, USA
117 York Street, Sydney, NSW 2000, Australia
100 Skyway Avenue, Toronto, Ontario, Canada M9W 3A6
Trio City, Coventry Street, Johannesburg 2001, South Africa
CML Centre, Queen & Wyndham, Auckland 1, New Zealand

Made and printed in Great Britain by
Richard Clay (The Chaucer Press) Ltd
Bungay, Suffolk
Set in Linotype Times

1

End of Tour

Impatient Virgin came to the target indicators nine minutes after midnight, at the fag-end of the third wave of Short Stirlings that had made up the Main Force. It was nobody's fault that they were late, but there had not been another reserve bomber operational at Slocombe Down when the flight engineer had noticed a fault in the fuel gauges as they were just on the point of leaving Dispersals; so the ground-crew had spent half an hour winkling out the gremlin in the electrical circuit.

The sergeant pilot had cut as many corners as he had dared on the outward track to Kassel, pushing the revolutions of the four Bristol Hercules engines to just below three thousand, so that the nacelles strained and creaked and the flight engineer nervously watched the flickering needles of the temperature gauges. The sergeant pilot had made time, it is true, but not quite enough time to integrate with the rest of the bomber stream in the lonely obscurity of the dying night.

They had not needed visual indicators to identify the target, which had become visible shortly after they had crossed the Dutch coast at Goedereede, for they could see the sinister glare of living destruction two hundred miles away. The sergeant pilot headed inexorably for the target, always racing against time, not even skirting the winking fighter beacons, in his desperate attempt to reach the comparative safety and anonymity of the bomber stream. And when at last they came to the flickering target indicators that glowed dimly within the cauldron of smoke and flame that marked the burning city, the sergeant pilot silently fought his urge to vomit, at the same time making a conscious effort to control the sudden muscular flabbiness in his knees and wrists.

The rest of the Stirling's crew had been silent and strained from the moment the Station Commander had confirmed that *Impatient Virgin*'s operation had not been scrubbed. Up to the target, their concentration had been fixed on the uneasy rhythm of the overtaxed engines, but now it switched to the glaring arena they had to cross, watching the blazing sky to left and right for any German Nightfighter flares.

Except for the tail-gunner this was their thirtieth operation as a crew. Because this completed their tour, the sergeant pilot had suppressed his urge to question the Station Commander's decision not to scrub. Tomorrow they should reach the dream beyond the nightmare and be off on leave. Although it was dodgy, they should be able to handle a late-arrival situation; they were after all an experienced crew.

'That's Kassel all right,' the navigator said. 'Lit up like Piccadilly Circus before the black-out.'

The co-pilot said:

'I don't much like the look of it. It seems too bloody empty to me. But then I never like it.'

The sergeant pilot fumbled for the red silk handkerchief his wife had given him last birthday when he was twenty-three. At an altitude higher than Mont Blanc he really had no business to have sweat beads on his forehead, in spite of the cabin heating; but for once the sergeant pilot had admitted his fear. He was afraid because they were alone, but his fear had increased when he failed to find the handkerchief which he carried on every trip; and that included the third Dortmund run when, after landing, they found the decapitated tail-gunner split neatly down his spine from neck to waist.

The sergeant pilot could feel the co-pilot looking at him and with a final nervous effort he pulled himself together, banking the Stirling round to the glimmer of the dying yellow pyrotechnic markers.

'O.K., Air Bomber. Almost time for the off.'

The flak suddenly rose to meet them as they made their bombing run, shaking and buffeting the aircraft as they left the doubtful safety of the darkness, where bomb loads were harmlessly burning out in the countryside, jettisoned by crews unable to face the inferno of fire they must meet on their approach.

'O.K., skipper, in and out in one.'

'It can't be quick enough for me, I can tell you. Make it a real knee-trembler.'

At his station in the upper turret, the sergeant air-gunner craned out and up through the polished turret Perspex, scanning the pink and emerald plumes of the cloud base, five thousand feet above. He was all too aware from the many photo-flash bromides he had seen pinned on the ladder, the morning after an operation, how the heavy bombers lumbered over the target vulnerably silhouetted against the raging fires below. Nightfighters could be watching *Impatient Virgin* under the cloud base above them. For a moment he froze, catching sight of a dot moving against the clouds, until he realized it was only a dirty mark on the Perspex.

As the Stirling buffeted and shook from the fire of the fifty-four heavy flak batteries that ringed the city, the rear-gunner swung his turret to left and right and depressed his quad Brownings in the indirect searchlight glare and the glow of the fires below. When he craned forward on the right-hand traverse, it was light enough to make out the irregular brown-and-green camouflage on the upper side of the port wing and the red and blue RAF roundel. He hated the half-light, willing the onset of the darkness once more, when night vision would be reduced to an uncertain one hundred yards. He kept telling himself that he did not want to die, not because he was frightened of death, but because time held so many unexplored possibilities.

Suddenly he caught sight of a white insect-like shadow six hundred yards astern.

'Nightfighter! Port! Dive! Go!' he shouted into the intercom.

A moment later he realized the enormity of their error as the Stirling plunged directly down into, instead of away from, the track of the attacking Nightfighter. The sergeant pilot, facing the nose, had turned to his port, which was starboard to the rear-gunner.

The rear-gunner began to scream incoherent curses as the proboscis nose of the Me Bf-110G waved and hovered uncertainly thirty feet below him, its nose gradually lifting. In his excitement the rear-gunner had also omitted to turn on his sight switch so that the sight graticule was lost in the blur of the Nightfighter's nose that merged with the surrounding darkness. He was already too late, as he groped for the master panel, blinded by the flash of the first eight cannon shells from the gun packs mounted above and below the Nightfighter's array of Lichtenstein and SN-2[1] radar aerials. The impact of the first of two of the cannon shells exploding against his shin-bone and the second within his chest cavity propelled his shattered corpse out of his safety belt and halfway through the metal doors of the rear entry port as a third shell ignited a flare. In a matter of seconds, the Frazer Nash turret was reduced to a chaos of flaring oxygen lines and exploding ammunition.

The Nightfighter's second salvo riddled the port wing-tanks, and a ricochet, having removed the co-pilot's index finger at the knuckle, also severed the port fuel lead just below the master engine cock, and the electrical fuel pumps continued to pour 100 octane petrol onto the cockpit floor at the rate of a gallon every twenty seconds.

By then the port wing-tanks were already alight, ignited by a blow-back of flame from the inner exhaust damper. Seconds later the petrol vapour trapped in the nose of the Stirling exploded with a roar and detonated the bomb load as the sergeant pilot still pressed the control column forward in a futile, instinctive dive.

Major Sepp Krasnatsky giggled as he felt the exploding red turbulence below him send his Me-110 skittering up towards the clouds. As usual, he had waited until the last possible moment before pulling back the stick to take his

[1] Luftwaffe airborne interception (radar) systems.

aircraft above and beyond the track of the stricken bomber. In the silence that followed he heard an audible sigh of relief from the other member of the crew and frowned.

'That makes a hundred and three. Another victory. A straggler. You should be glad of it.'

Hogel, the wireless operator, bit his lip. It had nothing to do with him. He had not been called upon to switch on the Lichtenstein set once that night, conditions over the city had been so perfect for visual attack.

'Any parachutes?'

'Nix, Herr Major.'

'Good. Victory. Total victory. Shot down in flames.'

Hogel could tell that the Major was adjusting his eye-patch, a trick he indulged in when he hit an emotional peak.

'Brown Bear sends congratulations,' Hogel said. 'The action has been followed on one of the Würzburgs.' The Major didn't seem to hear, as though the courtesy was irrelevant.

'They are giving us a new target in Dora Dora Two.'

'How kind of them,' Major Krasnatsky said, without turning his head. 'Well, I suppose we could just about make Vechta after shooting a couple more of the bastards down. Switch on the Lichtenstein, Hogel, and next time we'll share the victory laurels.'

2

Clixby Wolds

Although he was at last in bomber country, Sergeant pilot Hunting found the flat North Lincoln fenlands too bleak and level after the smooth wooded downs of his native Sussex. The Fenlands reflected the exposed nakedness of the night sky, the echo of its Roman roads straight and inevitable as a navigator's track along a Gee grid-plot.

However, at this moment, through the window of 'The

Plough', the flat inevitability was broken by a line of barrage balloons, seven miles to the north, marking the Humber defences around Kingston upon Hull. But it was not just North Sea shipping that was the target of Luftwaffe intrusion in 1943. Within the limits of their technical performance, the Heinkels and Dorniers struck and struck again at the airfields, rear bases and aircraft factories that formed Bomber Command's front line from the Wear to Hertfordshire. Only two days before, they had scattered anti-personnel butterfly bombs across the villages and farmland south of the Humber.

If for no other reason, therefore, the barrage balloons were logical enough even in such a countryside.

Meanwhile Hunting, still adjusting to the new posting to 241 Squadron, Clixby Wolds, observed the tensions that were gradually mounting as his crew faced their first tour of operations. With the sun shining outside, it seemed as good a time to start as any.

The others were grouped around the bar, subdued, like new boys on their first day at school, fully aware that although they were a crew, they were only a 'sprog' crew, untested and without any kind of battle experience together. Barton, the Australian tail-gunner, caught Hunting's eye:

'Having the other half, Cap?'

There was just the slightest undertone of uncertainty about the title. This was only partly because Barton himself was uncertain, not so much whether he would survive his first tour – all of them were aware that the odds were against them – but whether, when it came to it, they would weld together as a crew to increase their chances of survival. Together they formed a group of seven highly trained experts, mutually relying on one another's skill and ability, which, up to now, had not been tested against the harsh reality of operational flight over the Third Reich and Occupied Europe.

Although they had flown together often enough, clocking up something approaching 300 hours' flying time, that had only been on cross-country flights and night exercises. None of them could predict how Hunting would carry his heavy responsibility as pilot. In the next few days it would be the real thing. And then the officer was another factor.

Hunting looked round slowly before smiling his preoccupied smile.

'O.K. Might as well have one for the road.'

The WAAF sergeant standing beside Barton caught his smile and returned it. Hunting had known she was with Barton, but had not wanted to intrude on what seemed to be the start of an on-going romance. He knew that Barton had only been two days on the station before he had dated the WAAF sergeant.

'Sergeant Nicholls, this is our Cap, Sergeant Pilot Hunting.'

She smiled again as Hunting struggled for something appropriate:

'Sergeant Barton's a fast worker. I should watch him.'

'Don't worry, I like the positive approach.'

Barton said:

'There's no time to hang about in this war.' It had to be admitted that Sergeant Nicholls looked very decorative in her short skirt. Her fair hair was back-combed up in defiance of the prescribed and somewhat unfeminine Liberty Cut. Hunting presumed she got away with it because she was a sergeant.

As Barton turned away to order her a gin and lime, she added:

'If they have such a thing.'

Five other crew members were playing darts. Maitland, the navigator, had just scored a double top with bored precision, reducing his team's score to forty-one. His partner was Eddie Fairclough, the long-haired sergeant wireless operator. Maitland smiled his thin smile and said:

'Let's see if the upper turret gunner can beat that, without the excuse of the taboo track.'

On Lancasters and other aircraft with a rear upper turret, the tail plane was safeguarded against an inadvertent burst of .303 by an upward curving rail that carried the field of fire above it.

Trapper McIndoe took the darts and jabbed the first into eleven, wrinkling his eyes against the smoke from the Senior Service cigarette he habitually had in the corner of his mouth. However, his next throw was a triple nineteen, which blew the score.

'You had bloody well do better than that,' commented Fairclough, 'when a Junkers is homing in on our exhausts.'

'I can't work round the clock, not even for you, buddy. I have no day vision.'

Howells, the flight engineer, morosely chalked up the score as though, if he hadn't volunteered to supervise, he could have done much better himself and surprised them all. Standing beside a full beer glass, with the chalk delicately held so as not to dirty his fingers, he projected an air of aloof superiority.

'Besides,' McIndoe added, 'Fairclough's a gen kid. He's actually been inside a kite when shots have been fired in anger.'

Fairclough had remustered as bomber crew after two years of workings an AI radar in a Beaufighter. As a result, he was a silent encouragement to them all, besides being a gold-mine of information on radio-location. As an operator, he had more than once steered his pilot onto the track of intruding German bombers.

Fairclough smiled like a popular uncle behind his handle-bar moustache with the slightest hint of smugness, aware that the common knowledge of his past put him in a special position.

Hunting turned to watch the WAAF sergeant sipping her gin and lime while Barton made urgent conversation. It was clear that he wanted to monopolize her and at the same time show her off. She didn't seem to have the same idea exactly when she said across Barton in Hunting's direction:

'The poop from Group says you're for the off tomorrow night.'

For a moment Hunting was shocked by this open breach of security, since he was used to little admonitory posters that read: *Careless talk costs lives*. But after all, he reflected, there was nobody else but themselves in the dark little bar parlour with the foxed *Industry and Idleness* print on the wall, the varnished perch in a glass case and the 1942 calendar advertising Bainbridge's Poultry Nuggets. Even if they had the inclination, the farmworkers who would normally have used the public bar would be out planting potatoes. The only stranger was the landlord, his face as lined and creased as a balk of fenland oak; with his collarless shirt and rolled-up sleeves, he seemed an unlikely candidate for Fifth Column activities. In any case there was no phone.

Barton had reacted only slightly to the WAAF sergeant's news, clearly more concerned at making a favourable impression; the way that Sergeant Nicholls was answering him, it looked as though he was not without success.

'That's what we're here for. We've got a job to do.'

For a moment he seemed to shrink inside his dark-blue RAAF uniform despite his confident largeness, as the composite memory of his secure days with a Sydney accountancy firm flashed through his mind. Hunting himself shivered slightly and he gripped the edge of the bar, recalling his initiatory visits to the Third Reich, sitting hunched up on the second pilot's folding seat in the gangway between the flight engineer's station and the air bomber's compartment, in the role of 'second dicky'.

It was mandatory for all pilots to endure that unnerving experience and he had still not digested the boredom, confusion and helplessness of sitting squeezed in a corner, all too aware that he was not merely an outsider, but a Jonah, wished on a reluctant crew who resented any unpredictable additional factor that could militate against their own survival. It had been even more terrifying than he could ever have imagined; the more so since he was an observer with no useful or established role to play. On the way back from Essen on the second trip they had been caught in a searchlight cone north of Ghent, and Mattheson, the pilot, had put the Lancaster into a 300 mph dive, buffeting the tail plane so badly on recovery that Hunting had thought it would disintegrate.

Flying Officer Mattheson had given a clipped, perfunctory running commentary on what they had encountered, distinguishing light flak from heavy, and identifying the violet pencil beam of the radar-controlled master searchlights from the restless white light of ordinary batteries. From time to time he had identified German Nightfighter Beacons, smoke generators and decoy cities, but he had flown the aircraft with a kind of desperate recklessness that Hunting did not approve of. To the sergeant pilot the crew and its plane were a complementary and self-supporting unit, but he had the feeling that Flying Officer Mattheson hated the plane almost as much as he hated the crew, because they were both of them there and he could not avoid being involved with them and either or both could kill him.

Later at de-briefing he had learned it was Mattheson's seventeenth operation.

The WAAF sergeant said:

'It's almost certain gen. There'll be no moon, and the met reports are steady with just enough of the right kind of cloud.'

'What sort's that?' Barton asked and then said: 'I'm no weather wizard. It's all the same to me.'

'Not if your guns froze up on you.'

Flying through a comforting blanket of strato-cumulus at anything over 12,000 feet could produce icing, against which only key points of the Lancaster were protected.

Subdued by the future uncertainties he would have to face beyond any textbook training lecture, Barton gazed steadily into his pint glass.

Hunting joined in and asked Sergeant Nicholls:

'How do you know about the op?'

She patted Barton's sleeve:

'Don't worry, you'll be all right.' Then she answered Hunting's question:

'Everyone always knows from the Controller down. They always phone through the petrol and armament indent the day before and then it's confirmed. It's not very difficult to make an intelligent guess on the gallons asked for. High petrol load, low bomb load is Berlin. Low petrol load, high bomb load is the Ruhr. Group are pressing on to at least three or four ops a week now that the weather's getting better. Maximizing the maximum effort.'

Barton put down his empty glass and said:

'How good are you with a crystal ball?'

The WAAF sergeant didn't look him in the eye for some reason when she answered his question.

'Not my strong point, Sergeant, I'm afraid.'

Hunting, catching a slightly nervous resonance in her voice, wondered what she was really saying.

They were all of them volunteers, well aware of the risks they faced and that an average cumulative four to ten per cent aircraft loss on operations left them with a twenty-five per cent chance of survival over a thirty-trip tour. Crews had to be dead lucky to survive a tour; not many of them did.

Barton said:

'Anyway, I'm not interested in crystal balls. If your number's up, your number's up. I'd much sooner have it that way than Adolf voted in as P.M.'

None of them felt it necessary to make any further comment because they could only agree with him.

Suddenly Sergeant Nicholls got up to go.

'Thanks for the drink, Sergeant. I'm on watch at fourteen hundred, there's a new shift at the exchange.'

'I'll buy you another, when we get back.'

'All right.'

'And you will see us off, won't you? It'll be our first ride on the merry-go-round.'

'I know. I'll be thinking of you, even if I don't make it.'

'Maybe see you this evening then.'

'Maybe.' She bobbed out of the doorway after collecting her respirator case.

'We better be going too,' said Hunting. Suddenly he felt restless as though he couldn't wait another twenty-four hours. It was the kind of feeling he had had at grammar school before an important exam; it would be much better to take what was coming right away, so that it would be over and done with. But then there wasn't just one exam, there would be thirty. Some crews even did a second tour. A kind of postgraduate course.

'Where the hell's "Cranwell"?' Barton asked after the WAAF sergeant had left. 'Is he upstaging us or something?'

Hunting had been acutely aware of the one absent crew member, Pilot Officer Collins, the air bomber. It was a problem that he did not want to have on his mind just at that moment.

'He said something about having to sort out his mess bill.'

The divisions between officer and sergeant had not been fully worked out between them as yet. Hunting as pilot was captain of the crew regardless of the rank of others flying with him. Off duty, there were a number of areas that were less precisely defined. Officers normally went to one pub, sergeants to another. Barton had wondered whether Collins had been able to achieve any compromise so far as they were concerned.

When the crew had been made up in the last week at the Training Unit, Hunting had found himself short of an air bomber. The other sergeants had been keen to bring themselves to his notice, naturally gravitating towards him, since he had passed out high on the pilot's course. On the other hand Collins had not done sufficiently well to be rated either as pilot or navigator and, cast in the role of Pilot Officer Air Bomber, had not generated much enthusiasm from the sergeant pilots who would be captaining their own bombers.

Hunting had had his eye on Walpole as air bomber; he had done well on his course and seemed steady. However, at the final interview Walpole had decided that Bomber Command operations were not for him; a perfectly legitimate decision, even at that late stage, for it would have been impossible to turn back after his first posting. As a result Hunting was left with Collins alone to choose from. The Pilot Officer looked embarrassed as Hunting came up to him.

'Looking for a crew?'

'Yes, Sergeant.'

'Follow me. I need an air bomber.'

The rest of the sergeants in Hunting's crew were uneasy about this turn of events, not so much because Collins was an officer, although his exaggerated public school attitudes were often irritating, but because his performance might turn out to be less than adequate. They did not wish to risk their lives to Germany and back if the air bomber wasn't handy with a Mark XIVA bombsight.

Collins had tried his best to make himself agreeable and was always offering to buy them drinks, but that did not lessen their suspicions. He talked a totally different language from most of them, liked playing golf at Wentworth and was always trying to persuade them to play squash. Another irritant was the fact that he owned an M.G. sports car, which he used to further an apparently exotic love life in London and the neighbouring country clubs. Tension increased still further when they picked up their sergeant flight engineer from the HCU, for Howells had a fear and suspicion of officers that he made little attempt to conceal.

Barton said:

'Oh well, we'll see. I expect it'll be a perfect three point landing. "Cranwell" probably isn't such a bad chap, once you get to know him.'

In the circumstances Hunting was grateful for Barton's optimistic judgement.

'I expect so.'

After that, all six of them left the pub and began to cycle the mile and a half back to Clixby Wolds.

McIndoe, the keep-fit Canadian, was in front when they came to the crossroads where the signpost had been missing since 1940 to confuse German parachutists.

When McIndoe took the right-hand fork, Hunting was too far back to stop him. After fifty yards they left the copse that ran the length of the hill and the Canadian stopped at a sign stencilled '58MU'.

When they caught up with him they found the reason why he had dismounted. Aircraftsmen were painstakingly winching pieces of aircraft wreckage onto a 60-foot Queen

Mary low loader in the adjacent field.

To Hunting there didn't seem very much worth recovering from the burnt and shattered Lancaster that lay spread around a twenty-foot crater in a blackened field of winter wheat. Hunting walked over to where a flight sergeant was supervising a squad laying a track of railway sleepers across the ditch to make an improvised roadway for the Queen Mary low loader.

'Which way to Clixby Wolds, Flight?'

'You're off track, Sergeant. This is Audley Top and that there's Caen Hill. If you take the left-hand fork down the road, you'll hit the main gate in ten minutes.'

Hunting wanted to thank him and turn away but, riveted by the scene of destruction spread across the field, he could not resist the obvious question.

'What happened here then, Flight?'

The flight sergeant pulled heavily at his Woodbine and looked Hunting over as if confirming to himself that the sergeant pilot was wet behind the ears with his shiny new brevet and stripes.

'Nignog crew pranged on take-off. Their third op booked. That's what you're left with when thirteen tons of 100 octane and HE hit the deck. It happens every day. Sometimes I don't know why we bother, except the bits and pieces aren't good for civvy morale.'

Hunting took in more details of the wreck. As might be expected, the hundred-foot fuselage had snapped at each end of the bomb-bay and had been so gutted by fire that it was impossible to read the squadron markings. Only the rear gun-turret apparently remained intact and an armourer had already removed the quad .303 Brownings. The Merlin engines, their curved-back air-screws dug into the ground, had also survived, but there were only black holes in the wheat to show the former position of the four wing-tanks with their twenty-thousand-gallon capacity. The bomber's nose had been thrown forward by the force of the explosion, and the plexiglass of the upper turret and air bomber's windows were smoke-blackened and cracked. The blazing cargo of incendiaries had melted the aluminium formers and alloy wing root spars before the violence of the explosion had distributed them as chunks of shapeless metal throughout the copse and cornfield. At the same time, by some freak of dynamics, the dinghy had been thrown clear and had been inflated in the embracing branches of a beech tree where it remained, an incongruous yellow marker.

There were no obvious signs of the crew.

'Christ Almighty,' Hunting said. 'There isn't much left for the souvenir hunters.'

'There's fuck all left of anything. A total write-off, though maybe we could have the plugs reground. The kite got up to a thousand, dropped a wing and started to turn. After five revolutions that got more and more dicey, it hit the deck and pranged. The whole crew bought it. The four-thousand-pound cookie saw to that after the Lanc was drenched in petrol. Funny what some of these sergeant pilots pick up at Flying School.'

Pilot Officer Collins raised his hand in a perfunctory greeting to Hunting and Barton as he caught sight of them across the Ops Mess anteroom to a background of the Andrews Sisters:

'He was a master of his craft ...
But his number came up; he was caught in the draft ...
He's in the Army now, a-blowing reveille ...
He's the boogie-woogie bugle boy of Company B ...'

When they came over, Collins signalled a mess waiter. 'What ho! Here, let me grab a stooge. What are you chaps having?'

On this station the Ops Mess was neutral ground shared by all flying crew regardless of rank. At this stage of the war, this station commander had finally accepted that the shared emotional experience of the bomber crews was too strong to be broken by traditional and arbitrary divisions.

At Clixby Wolds Hunting's crew would eat, sleep and fly together. If they died together, which was more than likely, they would at least be united by this common bond which, while they lived, was intended to give them a sense of stability and common purpose.

Nevertheless, there was a curious transitory atmosphere surrounding the Ops Mess, partly due to the inexorable nightly comb-out among the operational crews.

Collins raised his glass and announced:

'Here's mud in old Nasty's eye.'

'Here's to,' said Barton.

There was an awkward silence until Collins said at last:

'By the way, you chaps, if you value your life, don't get involved with a very snappy popsy that answers to the name of Sergeant Nicholls.'

Hunting saw Barton stiffen.

'Why ever not?'

'Because she's the local chop girl, old horse. So don't go rummaging for the chink in her blackouts.'

Hunting didn't say anything, weighing up the situation and glancing between the two men. Clearly Collins was only trying to help in his usual unsubtle way and show that he cared for their survival as much as any of them.

'I'm not the superstitious type,' Barton said slowly.

'I certainly am. Anyway, I have it on the best authority, the Station Adjutant no less, that she's the Station jinx. The crews she waves goodbye to depart for the Fatherland never to return.'

'You don't believe that sort of thing surely?' Hunting asked.

'You ask around and you'll find plenty of chaps who do. She's known locally as the "Undertaker's daughter", and anyone she latches onto gets chopped even when it's a straightforward gardening trip, dropping mines off the Scheldt.'

Barton looked half-fearful and half-angry, clearly torn between his feelings for the attractive and leggy Sergeant Nicholls, loyalty to the crew and irritation at Collins' manner. At last he said:

'I bought her a grog as it happens.'

It was Collins' turn to look shaken.

'You don't say so.'

Hunting was beginning to feel angry with Collins for making such an issue out of something so trivial just before their first operation together. What made him angrier still was the knowledge that, as yet, he was too inexperienced to be able to tell just how trivial it was, although, of course, he knew that many air-crew developed little superstitions and rituals as a shaky insurance for survival. But above all he did not want Barton jumpy and upset first time out as rear-gunner. His performance could be crucial when they encountered Nightfighters.

'Are you keen on her or something, old man?'

'What if I am? As a matter of fact, I'm probably seeing her this evening, and not for the last time either, if I have anything to do with it. Something else you ought to know. I've also invited her to wave us off, first time out.'

'You did what?' Collins said incredulously. 'What about the rest of us?'

'Why don't you air your line-shooting somewhere else, Collins? What you're saying sounds like a lot of pommy crap to me. She's a nice girl. I like her.'

'Just a minute, old man. Think about us. Can't you put her on ice until she starts to get lucky, for all our sakes?'

'I'm not giving her the brush-off on your say-so just because of some silly rumour.'

Barton had gradually been turning a delicate shade of salmon pink during this conversation. The more Collins went on with his remarks, the more Barton resented it and the more determined he became to prevent anything from interfering with his building relationship with Sergeant Nicholls.

'Mind you, I'm not saying that she isn't a snappy-looking popsy. She could fool anyone who didn't have access to her crime sheet.'

Hunting recalled her momentary hesitation in the pub, realizing that she knew the score well enough. It must be a terrible thing to live with; something over which she could have no possible control.

The runway stretched flatly out to a distant curtain of giant T2 hangars through the Mess window. The sixteen operational Lancasters of 241 Squadron were standing in the middle distance at Dispersals. He decided to change the subject:

'We missed you at the pub.'

'Don't worry, I wasn't pulling rank,' Collins said awkwardly. 'I had to see a man about a dog.'

Hunting guessed that the Pilot Officer had had to endure some off-the-cuff rocket from the Wing Commander. Yesterday there had been an Officers' Mess Night from which sergeants were excluded, during the course of which Collins had apparently started to break up the furniture, ripping off a lavatory seat to serve as an appropriate picture frame for the Führer. And as yet Collins had not even arrived at a point of operational stress.

Hunting had not considered applying for a commission as a long-term objective since he had had his call-up papers a year before. Everyone he knew felt it their duty to fight in some arm and they were all quite clear as to why they were fighting. If the Axis won the fight, England and the rest of Europe would be reduced to slave states with an unending prospect of total submission to the Third Reich, while it redrew the map of the world and ruthlessly destroyed its enemies. There could be no argument about this after three years of bombing at home, invasion abroad, as well as rationing and convoy losses. To anyone who had remotely experienced it, there could be no question as to the power and malice of the Third Reich as it marched confidently forward from victory to victory.

After the B.E.F.'s retreat from France, underequipped and overshadowed by the perpetuated obsolete traditions and command structure and inadequate tactics of 1918, it was obvious to Hunting that Bomber Command was the only modern arm capable of bringing the war to Germany itself and even ending it. He joined the Royal Air Force to do just that. Whether he was an officer or not was a detail.

Although the sergeant pilot was on first name terms

with the rest of his crew, he still did not know what the B in front of Collins represented. For his part, Collins had now fallen into an uneasy off-duty familiarity, as though the present situation was a ludicrous mistake, in any case only temporary, and as though, once the war was over, everything would revert to a familiar and sensible pattern. In the meantime he intended to make the best of things and tolerate a tiresome equality, even though, when off duty, the rest of the crew conducted themselves like peasants.

When they sat down to lunch, Collins tried to mend his fences by talking pre-war test cricket with Barton, although Hunting did not join in since it was a subject that did not interest him. Instead, his eye lingered once more over the sinister, predatory silhouettes of the Lancaster bombers in their black night markings. He wondered which aircraft would be allocated to them, while the mess waiter put a plate of watery mulligatawny soup down in front of him, followed later by a plate of macaroni cheese with carrots to improve night sight.

3

Sahara

The Sahara Nightclub lay in the basement of number 246 *bis* Chaussée d'Ixelles in the heart of Brussels. On the whole Krasnatsky did not care for the Belgians any more than he liked Brussels. For one thing, the streets seemed permanently dirty and the people, although not unco-operative, projected a kind of slovenly, independent apathy that irritated him. It seemed quite right that such a nineteenth-century anachronism should be absorbed into the New Order to learn new and better ways.

In the meantime, at any rate, Belgium existed to supplement the iron and coal production of the Ruhr, to provide Luftwaffe Nightfighter stations, and generally to be made use of like the chamber pot under the bed in the first-floor room in the Hotel International which maintained intimate connections with the Sahara Nightclub below.

Krasnatsky knew the hotel's geography quite well by this time, almost as well as he knew the Nightfighter beacons across Europe, from the grubby green corridor lino to the naked light bulbs and the establishment's permanent staff. These consisted of Pauline, a Flemish farmer's daughter; Alouette, a Parisian refugee whose husband had been killed, shot down in a Potez 63-11 on reconnaissance over Sedan in 1940; Berthaline, a former novice from a Marist convent in Fécamp; and Irene, whose passport had been issued in Léopoldville.

The Luftwaffe Major found the Sahara the most agreeable of the Brussels establishments, although it was some distance from where he was stationed at Hainaut with III/181 Staffel, because it was not usually crammed with German service personnel from the Army of Occupation. When he had a night out in Brussels, he usually took Fritz Lange with him.

The two men had developed a unique relationship that had developed as they had pioneered their own nightfighting technique, flying as a pair in their own individual *Kette*.[1]

Where Krasnatsky projected a bluff earthy confidence over his eternal inner restlessness, Lange was cautious and sometimes even nervous, although this had nothing to do with fear. In fact they were almost diametrically opposed in character and looks. Krasnatsky with his one eye was white-haired, lean and dominating; Lange was swarthy, dark and withdrawn. Krasnatsky had been brought up in Prussia; Lange close to the Walchensee in the Bavarian Alps.

When they had been in Stukas pursuing the weary and beaten Australian and British divisions down the long road from Thessaloniki, Lange had covered Krasnatsky at the end of his dive when he suddenly came under attack from

[1] Formation of (usually) three aircraft within a Geschwader (squadron).

a lone Hurricane. Since that time Krasnatsky had proved to be the more ruthless and daring pilot when they had been transferred to Nightfighters, and the Major had chalked up over a hundred victories. Nevertheless, he was acutely aware of the debt that he owed Lange and had insisted that he should accompany him to Berlin when he was awarded his Knight's Cross.

Lange, if he did not bask in Krasnatsky's reflected glory, was at least prepared to play a secondary role because he admired the Major. He liked his confidence and daring and his dislike of authority, although he himself tended to adhere rigidly to Luftwaffe directives.

Although the Bavarian was not subject to the periodic fits of restlessness that drove Krasnatsky to the nearest bar or nightclub in his pursuit of girls, he recognized that this was the same restlessness that had made the Major an ace at twenty-five, a constant and urgent search for excitement.

Krasnatsky, in fact, tolerated Lange on these forays because he was a special case. He did not like comradeship overflowing into his sexual adventures. He was a gourmet rather than a glutton in that department, and it was the excitement of the chase as much as anything else that interested him.

Once, a raw extrovert Nightfighter Leutnant from their Geschwader[1] had made the mistake of trying to force his company on them at the Sahara and, worse still, wanted to buy everyone in the room champagne. Krasnatsky had giggled nervously before saying:

'We don't come here for a regimental sing-song and wine-tasting, but to do serious business. Just like an operation.'

When the Leutnant had protested, since he was mildly drunk, Krasnatsky giggled again before going on:

'But, my dear fellow, I'm serious about everything and that includes my love life. That's why I'm such a success.'

That night Krasnatsky, sitting beside Lange, had so far seen nobody that he knew, apart from the permanent staff, in the twenty-foot room with its barely concealed odour of spilled wine and stale cigarette smoke, and its

[1] Squadron.

dusty palms and subdued amber lighting. The girls were lined up as usual along the chromium bar rail in front of the rows of black-market bottles, trying to make the best of themselves and showing their legs. The sight of their naked backs and the gleaming satin dresses did nothing on that occasion to stimulate Krasnatsky's sexuality.

Lange sat impassively sipping a glass of brandy. He was really rather indifferent to women, at any rate the sort that patronized the Sahara, since he knew them to be mercenary little whores who gave very little in exchange for the money that obsessed them.

The fact that there was nothing very interesting going on did not concern Krasnatsky greatly; the Sahara was to some extent a habit with him and it was not entirely important whether he ended the evening in someone else's bed. It was a rather more relaxed form of night patrol where one might or might not score, one might be lucky or one might not.

Dressed in black satin, the large-bosomed Madame Julienne smiled maternally at the two young Nightfighters from behind the bar and Krasnatsky answered with a little wave. The only other people in the club were two Belgian businessmen, who talked earnestly in a corner, ignoring the girls. Madame Julienne smiled politely again at Krasnatsky, trying to gauge his mood. After a victory he seemed more remote and she guessed this was the case tonight.

'Customers,' Lange said as two SS officers came in with two pretty girls who looked as though they were playing truant from the top form of a nearby lycée. The girl on the right had powder-blue eyes and a greedy mouth and immediately glanced over to where Krasnatsky was sitting.

The Major giggled.

'They've established visual contact.'

The second, a dark-haired girl with black eyes and thin Latin eyebrows, absorbed the two airmen in a second under a sweep of her eyelashes.

'They're bored with the SS élite. That's for sure. A cutting-out operation is called for. You can have the dark one.'

'O.K.'

The two Obersturmführers wore *Germania* cuffbands. Lange said:

'On leave for Russland by the look of it.'

'That's just the place for them. Let's make it memorable for all of them.'

Krasnatsky giggled again and snapped his fingers at Berthaline when the party had finally sat down.

'Yes, Herr Major? You want me?'

'I want a Ricard and a message delivered. Bring me the whole bottle.'

Krasnatsky had the feeling he was going to enjoy himself. Pastis was a drink that he preferred since it contained predictable surprises. The clear liquid clouded to a misty milky green, like the moon under ideal nightfighting conditions, its sweetness balanced by the sharpness of the liquorice. Besides, pastis, though pleasantly stimulating and theoretically aphrodisiac, was not the sort of drink it was easy to get drunk on.

While Berthaline was away, Lange watched Krasnatsky carefully write out a note on the back of his visiting card that was destined for the new arrivals:

'Why don't you join us in a victory celebration?'

While the visiting card was being delivered, the Major stood up very correctly, clicked his heels and bowed. After a muttered conference in which the two SS officers appeared to be less than enthusiastic, the SS officer with an Armoured Division badge laughed and then shrugged, staring a little insolently at the two airmen. Krasnatsky giggled and waved, sensing a subtle, rising challenge, a hidden antagonism that quickened his pulse, as he felt the rising interest of the women. It was just like the perfect night attack where all or nothing could happen.

The SS officers came over and introduced themselves. Krasnatsky forgot their names while identifying the blonde girl as Claire and the dark girl as Emmeline. Lange smiled thoughtfully from the shadows.

'What are we drinking?' Krasnatsky enquired. 'Something to keep out the cold perhaps?'

'Schnapps for us,' said the tank man. 'Champagne for

the girls.'

Krasnatsky giggled as he gave the order, looking over the two young officers with a deceptive smile. He concluded that they were halfway there to a cutting-out operation. Claire, who had a very fine complexion and fair curly hair, kept on glancing at his eyepatch, while Emmeline, after darting a glance at his decorations, turned her attention to Lange.

'That's right. You'll need to keep the cold out where you're going to.'

'Don't worry, Herr Major, we've already been; Kharkov, the Don, Belgorod. You name it, we've been there. We know Russia all right.'

'You mean Army Group South? Ukraine?'

'I meant exactly what I said.' The tank officer answered sharply. Lange noted that he retained a fixed parade-ground expression as he banged the table with the flat of his hand for emphasis, though it only helped to release the rising antagonism.

The other officer with infantry piping scowled and said:

'By the sound of it you should know, Krasnatsky. Sounds as though you were born in the bloody place.'

Krasnatsky giggled:

'Although it's confusing, I'm a Prussian in actual fact.'

'Really? I wouldn't have believed it.'

Lange said:

'How are things in the Ukraine?'

'Pretty bloody, but at least we're in the front line fighting for Germany.'

Lange said:

'Nobody has the monopoly for that.'

Berthaline put down the tray with the glasses, the champagne cooler and finally the bottle of schnapps.

When the drinks had been poured, the tank officer said abruptly:

'I see you're wearing the Nightfighter's badge, Herr Major. What sort of victory are we supposed to be celebrating? The British Bomber Kommando's destruction of the Ruhr?'

Krasnatsky did not appear to hear him:

'Really, Claire, you have the most wonderful blue eyes. Just like the Baltic on a sunny day.'

He kissed her hand.

Lange said:

'I don't think he heard what you said. Actually, it's his hundred-and-third kill.'

'What do you do then? Hang about and load his pop-gun for him?'

Emmeline said:

'Really, Hans, you shouldn't say things like that. You boys must be jealous.' She smiled at Lange, revealing a line of gold teeth.

This really enraged the SS tank officer, who could by this time see quite clearly the way things were going.

Lange said:

'I'd like to show you how the Nightfighters do it, Emmeline. I promise you, you won't be disappointed.'

The tank man interrupted:

'So he's an ace. Well, after all, nobody minds free drinks, but I must say I'm glad it's only the Ivans that can get me out of bed. You have my personal sympathy, of course. Nightfighters have never been a corps d'élite exactly, and with his disability it's a surprise he even manages to locate the bomber stream at all.'

Krasnatsky smiled. Things were turning out rather well and it could become a really exciting evening. Glancing in the mirror, he saw his grave, monk-like face reflected, with its arched eyebrows, black eyepatch and thick white hair.

He raised his glass:

'To the heroes of Stalingrad.'

Even the girls hesitated and put down their glasses as they saw the expression on the faces of their escorts.

'I didn't hear that,' said the SS tank officer as Krasnatsky added more water to his Ricard.

The Major raised his glass again:

'What I meant to say was: to the Roumanians, Italians, Hungarians and the celebrated SS.'

The tank man exploded at this.

'If you go around insulting the Corps, you'll have to take what's coming. I want satisfaction.'

The girls looked frightened although they were obviously excited by what was happening.

Krasnatsky giggled.

'Any satisfaction you like, ladies and gentlemen.'

'All right. I'll see you outside the SS barracks tomorrow morning at nine, since it's obvious you have no immediate plans for defending the Reich. You *can* use a pistol, can't you?'

'Wait a minute,' Krasnatsky said slowly. 'Hang on! What we use to kill each other is very much up to me. I know that much about it.'

The SS infantry officer interrupted:

'He's quite right about that, Hans.'

The challenger shrugged.

'What's the difference? What's the proposition?'

Krasnatsky smiled:

'Nightfighters fight an unorthodox war, and the habit sticks. So far as I'm concerned, my face has suffered enough already, so that rules out sabres.' He giggled as he fingered his eyepatch. Then he fumbled in his pocket and pulled out three rounds of 7.92-mm cannon ammunition.

'Here's how. Time right away. Method like this.' Krasnatsky removed the wire from a champagne cork and proceeded to twist it tightly behind the flange of the cannon shell.

'This is the basic weapon. Lange here checks the ammunition. Then we each go to a separate table, hold the propellant end over a candle flame and aim at each other. Of course, in my aircraft these things are fired electrically, but I'm sure that heat will have much the same effect.'

The expression on the faces of the SS men froze as he lightly passed the round through the candle flame.

'What's biting you? It should be child's play after the stories that emerge from SS Cadet School. I thought you got special training in your Heroics Class, balancing live egg grenades on top of your steel helmets and waiting for them to burst.'

'It's unorthodox.'

'You mean it's risky. That's right. Three things can happen. The recoil from the propellant can send the case on a reciprocal track to the bullet, which has elements of danger. The bullet may find its intended target and explode. Or the shells could simply burst in our faces.'

Krasnatsky took a sip of Ricard and then went on:

'Courage should be tested in unpredictable situations. I should know. Everyone tries to kill me – our flak, the enemy bombers, my own crew, my own plane, the weather. But you see I continue to kill the British in quantity, which is why they give me jewellery to wear.' He touched the ribbon of his Knight's Cross.

The two SS men glanced at each other doubtfully; the girls looked at Krasnatsky in open adoration.

Lange took up a round and again slowly drew it over the candle flame.

'One would have to hold it there for quite some time to get results. The propellant would only ignite at about four hundred degrees.'

The SS tank officer was sweating.

'It's mad.'

Krasnatsky giggled.

'But it's easy. Don't tell me you've lost interest before we've even begun.'

'The risks are unacceptable. It could involve others. In any case, I prefer to reserve my life for death on the battlefield.'

'All right. Well, let's leave it at that. I can't say I blame you. Knocking out obsolete Russian armour must seem fairly straightforward by comparison.'

The two SS men got up without saying another word. Krasnatsky laughed again and then said:

'But I'm not altogether sure if the girls want to leave. Or do they? They haven't seen anything yet.'

Claire and Emmeline smiled, but made no move. The SS men hesitated but they realized that they had already lost face. Krasnatsky had made his point and won the moral victory. He poured what champagne was left into the two girls' glasses and ordered another bottle.

'Good luck on the East Front,' Lange called to the two Obersturmführers as they made their way out.

Krasnatsky, for his part, did not waste any further time on romantic preliminaries once they had the two Belgian girls in the bedroom of the Hotel International. Putting down the bottle of Ricard, he pushed the angrily protesting Claire onto the bed and, throwing up her pleated skirt, revealed a pair of plain pink cotton pants decorated with stylized roses. She had dyed her legs brown, since stockings, even for her, were unobtainable. Her skin was tender and smooth and he noticed that it hardly darkened as he pushed his way into her vagina to one side of her pants.

In spite of Claire's angry protests he could tell that she had been sexually aroused by the ease with which the tip of his penis penetrated to the neck of her womb without difficulty. When this happened she relaxed, lying back, her nipples swelling and her eyes half-closed, with her right hand raised and slightly clenched. Then she began to respond to the rhythm of his heavy strokes, panting and revolving her hips round his penis, her open legs loosely bent on either side of him.

At first Emmeline had joined in Claire's outraged protests, adding her own comments of shocked disapproval at Krasnatsky's impetuous love-making.

Lange had started to calm her down:

'The Major's like that. He does everything on the spur of the moment.'

'How about you?'

'I take my time.'

Emmeline shrugged and walked round to watch the other couple on the double bed in a half-envious, but calculating way. As she bent over them, Lange raised her skirt from behind and, finding that she was not wearing any pants, slid his penis into her dark tuft of pubic hair from behind. Emmeline clutched the bed head and moaned. Then, with one hand, she unbuttoned the front of her blouse so that her breasts hung in front of Krasnatsky's face.

As a result Krasnatsky found his attention divided between Claire's sinuous movements, Emmeline's expression of intense pleasure and his own pleasure as he worked his penis in and out of Claire. Emmeline was quick to observe the effect that she was having on Krasnatsky and shakily puffed the smoke of the cigarette that she had lit into Krasnatsky's face.

'How about doing me a favour at the same time?'

'What's the matter? Can't you wait? You seem fully occupied to me. You should be. Lange's quite an expert.'

'It's not me I'm worried about.' She lowered her breasts in front of Krasnatsky's face.

After a moment Claire began to realize what Emmeline was up to as she began to moan, her breasts stiffened and the nipples grew erect.

'Wait your bloody turn,' she said tugging at Emmeline's thighs.

This only had the effect of making Emmeline kneel down on the bed, and the sight of her dark stockings, long dark pubic hair and pink rump raised to give deeper penetration to Lange excited him so much that he toppled over on her and gripped her breasts, working away until both of them reached a climax.

Krasnatsky suddenly stopped.

'What's the matter, Herr Major?' Claire asked, as she pushed away Emmeline who had collapsed to one side of her.

'Nothing's the matter. I need a cigarette, that's all.' He took the cigarette that was still burning from Emmeline's hand, feeling the same kind of tight excitement inside him as he did when he first made visual contact with an enemy bomber. The feeling was a curious mixture of anticipation and power. These two little girls were just as vulnerable as a Halifax or Stirling that, however it weaved and turned, knew that it had to be shot down in the end. The only difference was pleasure instead of pain. Life instead of death.

While Lange poured himself a drink and began to look

at Claire, Krasnatsky moved over the leg of the apparently unconscious Emmeline, noting that the area round her mouth was blotched with lipstick. She made no attempt to move as he pushed his penis inside her.

Lange immediately removed Claire's pants and mounted her, her hands clutching at her thighs and her stomach muscles rippling in desire. As Lange entered her, the muscles inside her vagina suddenly and unexpectedly contracted so that the pleasure she induced finally broke Lange's self-control and he plunged wildly into her in orgasm.

Emmeline lay unmoving in exactly the same attitude of eroticism in which Krasnatsky had entered her, her skirt half-hiding her pubic hair. Only her hands moved, fondling Krasnatsky's balls.

When Krasnatsky came, it was like the time that he overshot the Halifax over Stuttgart so that the force of the explosion lit up the sky with a deafening roar and an engine cowling clattered against his tail plane and he went into an involuntary spin, the lights of the flickering city below revolving against pieces of falling wreckage. For a moment he lost control of the stick, which swung backwards and forwards, juddering wildly. When he opened his eyes, he found he was looking at the smile of animal satisfaction on Emmeline's face.

He got up and refilled his glass from the Ricard bottle and, after putting on his trousers, sat down in the easy-chair to inspect the wreckage of the battlefield.

He raised his glass:

'Victory. Total victory. Shot down in flames.'

Emmeline retained her smile of animal satisfaction, making no attempt to adjust her skirt, so that her exposed thighs continued their open invitation.

Claire knelt on the bed, making no attempt to get dressed, as she asked:

'What d'you mean: shot down in flames?'

Lange said:

'It's what we say in the Luftwaffe when we've scored a victory.'

'I can tell his gun's still loaded. Why doesn't he shoot me down in flames?'

Krasnatsky giggled nervously:

'Because I always aim to conserve my ammunition. I use Fritz there as a back-up on the job.'

'I don't understand.'

'Two bombers, two Nightfighters. One can't be everywhere at once. One's got to play it by ear. Lange and I work as a team.'

'You can say that again.'

Emmeline, catching sight of herself in the mirror, reached for her handbag and began to make herself up, still holding the same erotic position.

Claire lit a cigarette.

'What would have happened if you'd held one of those bullets over a candle?'

'God knows,' said Lange. 'But then, your SS boy friends hadn't tried it either. At least we brought the evening to a satisfying climax.'

Claire smiled, dropping her head onto her knees before finally bursting into fits of laughter. 'I think we deserve an award of the Knight's Cross after what happened tonight.'

4

Test Flight

That morning Hunting's crew was allocated P for Peter, and Howells signed the RAF 700 before they went off on a height test-flight.

P for Peter wasn't much to look at from the outside, which was not surprising since it was a composite aircraft made up from sections from four different planes which had ended their individual lives at Salvage Disposal, Cowley. The device on the nose had been crudely painted by some now forgotten crew and given the alternative name: *The Reaper of the Rhine.* The picture showed a skeleton heaving two five-hundred-pound bombs at a German schloss marked with a swastika. Hunting did not like it at all; although the aircraft had actually returned, the fact that it had required massive surgery did not encourage him. He considered the name to be meaningless and no longer applicable to the rebuilt Lancaster.

He was all in favour of having the name obliterated, but nobody else seemed to care one way or the other until Howells said lugubriously:

'I should leave it alone, if I were you. Changes can bring bad luck.'

'Why have a name at all? Other crews will be flying P for Peter. I just don't fancy starting the first op in a second-hand Lanc with a death's head all over it. After all, we're not competing with the United States Eighth Air Force to come up with the sexiest pin-up.'

Barton said:

'I think the Cap's got a point. Let's start off with a clean sheet and have the sod painted out. We'll just stencil on a bomb for every op we chalk up.'

From then on their Lancaster was simply known as P for Peter.

The crew grouped round the rear starboard fuselage door, waiting to take up their stations, the air-gunners in their clumsy heated suits, as Hunting said to Howells:

'Have you made the outside check?'

'No, I've always left that to the ground-crew.'

'I never leave anything that involves my life and personal safety to anybody if I can avoid it.'

Hunting turned to the maintenance chiefie and asked him:

'Have your boys screwed down both leading edge inspection panels?'

'I'll have it checked for you, Sergeant.'

Hunting said:

'Don't worry about it. I'll take a look.'

He climbed the ladder by the servicing frame to the forward starboard wing root. A hinge ran from the inner nacelle, a foot behind the leading edge, giving access to the cabin air heat system. This servicing flap was secured by a line of screws at the leading edge. The panel gave slightly at his touch when he pushed it and when he looked closely, he found that a bolt was missing.

Hunting sucked in his cheeks in suppressed anger; an unsecured cowling or panel could fly loose on take-off, acting as an unstable air-brake which could make the Lancaster yaw, side-slip and crash.

The sergeant pilot climbed slowly down the servicing frame.

'I would give us a fifty-fifty chance on that one. You recall what someone once said, Chiefie? "Aviation is not unsafe, but like the sea it's terribly unforgiving of any carelessness or neglect."'

'I'm sorry, Sergeant. I'll put the fitter that's responsible on a fizzer.'

'That's up to you. All I'm asking for is that the dice aren't loaded against us from the start.'

Hunting then checked that the Pitot tube hoods had been removed. The Pitot tube measured air-speed and monitored the barometric pressure which the altimeter registered as variations in height. Hunting also checked the five-foot-diameter tyres for creep. Although they were not new, they were not burned out.

When he was satisfied, he led the way up the metal ladder and through the rear starboard fuselage door and they took up their stations. The design of the Lancaster was such that five of the crew were stationed forward of the wing in the main cabin, leaving the rear and upper turret-gunners in comparative isolation in the rear two-thirds of the plane.

Hunting sat down on his parachute on the bucket seat facing the controls and started the first engine. When all four Merlins were running, the ground-crew screwed down the priming pumps in the inboard nacelles and removed the ground battery. Hunting opened the throttles in turn of each of the four Merlin XX engines that generated over a thousand horsepower, gradually increasing the revolutions to 1,200. The air-screws whistled and shook the wings and the airframe, as Hunting then checked the hydraulics by raising and lowering the flaps and opening and shutting the bomb doors.

Next he checked the altimeter setting and adjusted it to the correct QFE millibar reading Maitland had passed to him; the airfield at Clixby Wolds was three hundred and thirty feet above sea-level.

Meanwhile, as Hunting pulled out the master engine cock, opened the radiator shutters and turned the superchargers to mod, Howells at the flight engineer's panel switched the fuel tank selector to number 2 tank and flicked on the booster pump.

Hunting slowly released the brake lever below the port windscreen and the Lancaster taxied forward, its tail-wheel bumping over the ridges in the concrete sections leading away from Dispersals, the wings dipping under the weight of the engine nacelles and the airframe throbbing.

As the Aldis flashed green from the Watch Office, Hunting opened the throttles to zero boost against the brakes and finding that the engines responded evenly, throttled back and released the brakes once more. Then he gently increased power again, advancing the port throttles to counter any tendency to swing. By the time that Howells had advanced the throttles to maximum power, the Lancaster had already travelled five hundred yards at an increasing velocity down the runway to just under a hundred miles an hour, when the sergeant pilot eased forward the control column to bring up the tail and then drew it back between his knees.

Maitland entered in the navigator's log:

'10.36 hours. Airborne.'

At five hundred feet Hunting raised the flaps and corrected the resultant forward nose-down trim.

Against the roar of the engines, Hunting flicked the R/T switch moulded into his oxygen mask and said to Maitland:

'I'm setting course for Grimsby, Professor, and I'll check with you when I think we've hit it.'

They had already left the sombre darkened landscape and the faint runway criss-cross of Clixby Wolds that lay under the blanket of cumulus which hovered loweringly over the Lincoln Fens and across to the coast. Soon they were nosing through it, suddenly caught in the nebulous ghost world which even seemed to soften the roar of the engines. Climbing at 160 mph, they should be over Grimsby in five minutes, before starting their long thirty-five minute haul to 20,000 feet. In fact, the force 3 tail wind predicted by Met should clip a minute off the time.

'Everyone O.K.?' Hunting asked. There was no reply. Hunting thought, they are still getting used to it all.

The twin green lights disappeared from the control panel as he eased the undercarriage control lever back and the wheels retracted with a clump into the inner nacelles.

Forward of Hunting, in the nose bubble of the aircraft, his elbows resting on the padded step beside the Mark XIV bombsight, 'Cranwell' Collins lay sprawled, his left leg touching the bombsight computer, the size of a medium attaché-case. The computer was powered from the port inner generator which worked the RAE compressor and the vacuum pump operating the gyros. From information supplied by the air speed indicator, altimeter and sighting head, the computer fed back constantly adjusted sighting and drift angles to the air bomber.

At that moment this was no concern of Pilot Officer Collins whose mind was occupied with the thought that the 'Yankee Clippers', a US Eighth Army Jazz Band, were performing at a services dance in three days' time. The air bomber was a jazz fan and had been trying to find out at the Station whether Saturday flying tended to be scrubbed in the interests of a quiet week-end. Above the flat angled air bomber's window was positioned the forward Frazer Nash turret, its circular hatch leading to the twinned .303 Browning machine-guns for frontal defence.

Collins had no intention of occupying the cramped, uncomfortable gunner's seat unless he had to, his thighs stretched over the emergency exit panel, that took up half the floor space in the bombing compartment. This was the officially recommended point of emergency exit for all the crew.

Behind him and up three steps that lay beside the Mark IV automatic pilot, the nose opened up into the main crew compartment where the green paint suddenly became scratched and faded.

Off centre and to the left as one looked forward lay the pilot's station and the instrument panel. Behind and to the right, Howells sat watching the square black flight engineer's panel, on which the top dials were banked in fours to monitor the oil and coolant temperatures on each individual engine. The lowest six dials recorded the fuel contents of the six wing-tanks, with their maximum combined load of 2,154 gallons of high octane fuel. At this moment Howells was carefully watching the bank of fuel-pressure warning lights, a flicker from which might signal fuel starvation during the climb. As he glanced over the instruments minute by minute, he also thought how much he would like to be a pilot.

He could never quite understand how it was that he had not been selected for flying training from the start, eventually, somewhat sourly, putting it down to the fact that he had only been through the ATC and had none of the advantages of passing through a University Air Squadron. He was unaware that Hunting had had neither advantage. However, Howells was inclined to be a bitter man, projecting his own uncertainties onto others, disguised as righteous resentment at an apparently unfair world. In some ways his attitude was justified. His wife Emily was still suffering from the anxiety neurosis induced by six days' continuous bombing on Teesside.

'Professor' Maitland worked on meticulously at the navigator's station below the astrodome, sitting with his back to Howells, the beam of his Anglepoise lamp concentrated on the half-inch map of Lincolnshire beside his Hughes protractor, dividers, compass rose and circular slide-rule. Also to hand was his computer, an aid to solving that eternal navigational problem, the triangle of velocities. Arranged above the table was Gee, the long rectangular units containing the navigational radar next to the backs of Monica and Boozer – defensive radars – controlled from the wireless operator's station behind.

As was to be expected of an ex-schoolmaster, his log was as carefully kept as copies of his school reports. His handwriting, however, revealed a certain immaturity, which showed in the attitude that he knew best about most things. He had joined the RAF to fill in time before taking up a place at Clare College, Cambridge. Sometimes he felt that the war was going on for so long it was beginning to threaten his career.

Behind the armour-plate bulkhead that ran three-quarters of the way across the fuselage to the left of the navigator's table and just before the wing root, lay the wireless operator's station. The equipment for which Eddie Fairclough was responsible consisted of the T 1154/R 1155 transmitter receiver; a receiver connected with the direction-finding loop below the canopy; receivers for blind approach, main and marker beacons. He could send either R/T, that is to say plain language, or morse.

In addition to Monica and Boozer there was some other specialized equipment: Tinsel – a transmitter for jamming enemy fighter frequencies with relayed engine noise, and IFF to identify the aircraft as friendly to British radar-controlled ack-ack sites and nightfighters.

Fairclough was not over-enthusiastic about the equipment he had to work, since he would have very much preferred to have remustered as a radar navigator. He found his present job undemanding technically after operating A.I.

Directly behind him, the way back was interrupted by two low steps, formed by the intersection of the two main spars from the port and starboard wings behind the cabin heater intake. At this point the wings extended fifty-one feet on either side, carrying their load of wing-tanks and engines. At this point oxygen cylinders were clamped to the fuselage below the oxygen lines that ran fore and aft to service the crew at high altitudes. Between the mainspar intersections lay the stretcher or rest bed, depending on how you looked at it. Parallel to the oxygen lines were round conduits carrying the rudder and elevator control cables back along the remaining thirty-five feet of fuselage wall. They were joined, aft of the flare-chute, by the ammunition beltways for the rear turret-gunner's Brownings.

Arranged in parallel racks below the small oblong rear-fuselage windows were flares, a crash axe and a first-aid box.

Halfway along this fuselage end-section, McIndoe sat in the upper gun-turret with the curious suspended sensation he always felt as the clouds rushed by him in dark and light patches; puffy miniature cauliflowers of cumulus. There seemed to be a lot of buffeting and a lively tail wind.

Barton sat in the rear gun-turret between the twin rudders of the tail plane, its span only four feet less than the wingspan of a Spitfire, behind his quad .303 Brownings in the loneliest and most hazardous station of them all. It was from the rear that most Nightfighter attacks would materialize. That, for the moment at any rate, was academic, but all the buffeting had made him feel air-sick. Air-sickness had always been a secret problem with him, in spite of the hours he had put in. However, he had never felt quite as bad as this before. He could only hope that he would get over it, once they started operations.

Suddenly, through an angle of the clouds, he caught the unmistakable surge of white-capped waves in slow motion.

'I say, Cap. We're over the drink.'

Hunting reacted immediately:

'How do you read that, Professor?'

'It's impossible to tell without a fix. The tail wind may have picked up to force 6.'

Hunting said:

'That could add anything up to 30 mph to our track.'

Eddie Fairclough chipped in over the intercom:

'Some more bad news. I'll have to change the fuse on the transmitter, an HT surge must have blown it. Trev Howells needs to get the generator looked at.'

'I don't like it,' said Hunting. 'I'm not stooging about here waiting for you all to extract your digits. I'm going down to take a look.'

'For God's sake be careful, Cap,' said Maitland. 'The Humber's a shipping lane, a prohibited zone.'

'You should have thought of that before you took me halfway across the North Sea.'

Keeping his eye on the altimeter, which now registered 3250 feet, Hunting pushed the control column forward in a shallow dive. 1500 feet lower, two miles north-east and thirty seconds later, P for Peter emerged from the cloud base as Hunting dropped the starboard wing and eased the Lancaster into a long, low bank.

Lieutenant-Commander Penryn RNVR had been with the watch on the bridge of HMS *Petunia* for almost eleven hours, ever since his Flower class corvette had begun patiently to circle the fishing trawler *Scunthorpe Knight* as she moved forward uncertainly at ten knots, one of her screws fouled by a paravane wire some miles north-west of the Dogger.

The Lieutenant-Commander had been more than content to see the red and white landfall buoy at Sand Haile, marking the port Humber Channel. Soon they would have the protection of the Spurn Head batteries, and then he could stand down and leave the river pilotage to his Number One.

'I know one thing, Jimmy, and that's for sure. I'm having dinner and a hot bath at the Royal Hotel tonight after this morning's little drama, even if there's only Woolton pie on the menu.'

'Pity there's no Hatchett's in Hull.'

'Anything's better than this.'

As he spoke, he suddenly became aware of the throbbing roar and black silhouette of a four-engined bomber. After hours of scarcely relieved cold and boredom the duffel-coated gun-crews had seen it too and welcomed the Focke-Wulf Kondor for a target. The four oerlikons on the bridge wings spat out two hundred shells in silvery tracer arcs ahead of the oncoming aircraft.

P for Peter reeled from the blast of the explosions drifting by in cotton-wool puffs of black smoke, the Lancaster's airframe skin rippling and crackling with stress.

'Wizard show,' said Collins sarcastically. 'Right bang slap in the middle of the Hull Defence Zone. I couldn't have done better myself.'

'Don't kid yourself,' Hunting answered. 'I'm getting back to Clixby Wolds before anything else happens. Eddie, you'd better switch on the IFF. We don't want anyone else imitating that ship.'

'Better keep clear of Grimsby too.'

It was black and lowering below the cloud base as Hunting turned west and crossed the LNER railway line at Waltham.

Maitland entered in the navigator's log:

'10.43 hrs. Attacked in error by Naval escort vessel in Humber Estuary. No damage sustained.'

Ten minutes later, Hunting made his final approach, less than enthusiastic with the morning's work. On a fifteen-minute test-flight they had been dead lucky to avoid serious trouble and that was largely due to Barton. He trembled to think what was likely to happen on their way to and from the Third Reich. He would rate their survival chances as five to one against on current form.

After the Lancaster had landed, Hunting raised the flaps and opened the radiator shutters before switching off the outer engines to taxi back to Dispersals. Once he had stopped, he opened the bomb doors, switched off the inner engines and disconnected the electrics.

Somewhat to his surprise, Chiefie and his maintenance crew were there to greet him.

'What's up?'

'You're on tonight, Sergeant. The crew lists have been posted.'

Hunting felt the muscles tighten across his stomach.

'We didn't make it up to twenty thousand.'

'I thought you were quick. What was the trouble?'

'Nothing to do with the aircraft. I just decided to scrub it.'

'It's lucky you did, Sergeant. The armourers want to start bombing up.'

'Well, anyway, the R.T.'s u/s. The generator needs adjustment.'

'Leave it to me. I'll put a sparks on it right away. See you later. We've a lot to do.'

The crew walked away from Dispersals towards the huts. Hunting thought Barton seemed rather white and wondered if it had anything to do with Sergeant Nicholls.

The roneoed crew list was pinned next to Daily Orders and all their names were there. All told, the Squadron was putting up fourteen Lancasters. Below the crew lists was the timetable of the afternoon's events. It all seemed so casual somehow, Hunting thought.

Navigator's briefing	1500
Main briefing	1600
Meal	1700
Final briefing	1800
Take-off	1900

As soon as he had read it, Barton wondered whether he would be able to see Sergeant Nicholls. He was already feeling better once they were down. He had found out that her first name was Angela, but he still thought of her as Sergeant Nicholls. It seemed more appropriate somehow.

5

The Briefing

The trouble with Pilot Officer Collins was not that he was a coward – he was too insensitive to be that consciously – but that he had never been in a situation, so far as he was concerned, that proved that he was not.

That was not to say that he had not tried various dangerous experiments such as rock climbing, but when he got to Llanberis Pass below Snowdon, there had always been some obstacle which, in his opinion, prevented him from testing himself to the limit.

One of these was his body. He was large and heavy, but with short arms, which meant that, although he could be just about pulled up more the arduous routes like Cenotaph Corner on Dinas Cromlech, he lacked the strength and reach to pioneer new routes. His failure to be able to extend his fingertips an inch meant that a thin flake of rock, the only possible means of advancing up the 180° rock face was as far away as the other side of the valley.

It was for this reason that Collins felt concern when it became clear that the Australian rear-gunner was not going to close the book in Sergeant Nicholls' direction, since this somehow seemed to shorten the odds against learning the truth about himself, as he did not wish to conduct his self-imposed test for bravery with too much outside interference.

As it was, he felt he would soon find out, since an operational tour on Bomber Command was unlikely to be without incident, which was the basic reason why he had volunteered, realizing that the experience would test his sang-froid and manhood to the full. But now it was too late for him to back out, and the flight of P for Peter across, into and away from Germany was as inevitable as this evening's sunset.

What made it all the more important for Collins was that he was an officer, and therefore a leader, who must always be ready to demonstrate even more courage and risk his person for the common good. As things had turned out, the rest of the Lancaster crew were sergeants, whether through lack of ambition or character defect, it was impossible to say. They all seemed normal enough to him, which in a way made his predicament worse.

Graded as air bomber, Collins was particularly infuriated with himself when he realized that two NCOs should have rated the more demanding functions of pilot and navigator.

The only way he could redeem his failure in his own eyes was by demonstrating a high measure of officer qualities including extra determination, resourcefulness and, above all, courage, and of course this was the one quality he was not sure he possessed.

The Briefing Room stretched out on either side of Collins, like the starting gate in the race to prove himself once and for all.

The pilot officer, waiting with the hundred others for the arrival of the squadron commander and his staff, tried to read the faces of the other experienced crews to see whether he could establish any difference in their expressions which set them apart from himself.

Beside him, Hunting was also glancing across the faces of the waiting crews as though he too was searching for the secret signs of survival. Some crews were confident; others were tight-lipped, anxious and nervous.

Collins noticed that Barton was missing and was about to comment on the fact when his eye caught a large notice pinned to the wall of the Nissen hut:

'It is better to keep your mouth shut and let people think you're a fool than to open it and remove all doubt.'

For a moment the pilot officer picked up the uneasy transit-like atmosphere of the Briefing Room. The message was addressed to bumptious new boys, and there would always be keen new boys, full to the brim with stupid questions which only experience would answer. Tonight it was their turn. He was just another new boy with one ring on his sleeve.

They all got up and stood to attention when Thornton, the squadron commander, walked down the centre aisle accompanied by his briefing entourage of intelligence, met, signals and armaments officers. He brushed past the epidiascope projector on the dais and stopped in front of the unveiled route and the target maps. The security precaution which dictated that the maps should remain concealed up to the last possible moment, an unknown question mark, inevitably made them the centre of dramatic focus. The fate of all the crews was written behind the camouflage of empty white sheets of paper. Just like the future, it was unknowable until it happened.

The target map would show whether they would be attacking an 'easy' target outside Germany, which would earn them only a third of an operation to count towards their tour, or whether they would be dicing with death past the Luftwaffe Nightfighter beacons all the way to Berlin.

'O.K. Sit down,' said the squadron commander. 'You may smoke.'

Looking round him again as the room relaxed into its uneasy expectation, Collins was once more aware of the feeling of a railway station waiting-room on the line to nowhere.

Thornton, the twenty-five-year-old squadron commander, a veteran of fifty-three operations and with the DFC ribbon up, announced, looking through the wall behind the waiting crews:

'The target tonight is Emsdorf. Code name Whiting.'

He glanced quickly over the assembled crews, instantly summing up their mood, so that he could tailor what he had to say to fit it.

A slight murmur ran through the room and someone at the back shouted:

'Turn right at Liège and watch out for the heavy flak.'

The room laughed, relieving the tension, but only slightly. It could have been worse, Leipzig or Jena. Emsdorf was a hundred miles inside Germany and some of the crews knew the target, which gave them an increased sense of confidence. In the interval, the intelligence sergeant had removed the pins of the covering sheets and unveiled the scale 1/1000 000 flight map. A red ribbon stabbed out of Lincolnshire to Walcheren and then south-east over the Ardennes and the Rhine towards Hesse.

'The target is Emsdorf, maximum effort. As we should all know by this time, there are many industrial targets which supply components to the German aircraft industry. Not forgetting that the usual object of the exercise is to de-house as many war-workers as possible. Last time, the Wycombe Abbey Photo Unit gave you three out of ten for destruction, a score that they want you to improve on. It's very much up to you. If you don't want a return trip to Emsdorf, make a good job of it this time. Group continue to be concerned about the creep-back disease away from the target indicators, and so am I. Press on regardless and destroy the target. I don't want to have to deal with any more rabbit crews.'

He paused and took a sip from the glass of water on the rostrum.

'81 Pathfinder Squadron are laying a yellow ground-marker outside Friedberg at 1136 hours. A bearing of 114 south-east will take you ten miles to the red target indicators which will be dropped at 1146 hours and backed up every four minutes. If met is against you, and I am told this is unlikely, there will be Newhaven skymarkers over the target. We are in Main Force first wave with the rest of One Group, and the predicted force will amount to 862 heavy bombers. Bombing for first-wave Lancasters will be at 20,000 feet. Plaster it, chaps, and make a really good job of it this time. Wipe it off the bloody map, in fact.'

Maitland was busy checking the notes he had already taken at the navigators' briefing, an hour earlier, as the intelligence officer stepped forward.

'Course bearings are on the navigators' notes, but you can see the general form from the Ordnance Survey.' He tapped the map. 'Air bombers will draw target maps immediately after this briefing. Kindly note the river bridges which are an important signpost. There are five of them.

Now look at the opposition map.'

There were catcalls and sarcastic cheers.

'One, the coastal searchlight and ack-ack belt; we know all about that. Watch out for the railways north of Brussels. There's been a report that Jerry may have mobile ack-ack. So far as the Luftwaffe is concerned, the outward bomber stream will be passing between St Trond and Venlo not far from Beacon Bazi, so watch out for Nightfighters. Nearer the target keep to the south of that well-known bogey hole, Koblenz. So far as Emsdorf is concerned, it is a moderately defended target so you can expect a reception committee of light, medium and heavy flak. We have identified at least five heavy batteries. There may also be balloons, so don't start weaving about at zero feet unless you have to.'

There was a sarcastic groan which he allowed to subside before continuing.

'We are laying on two spoofs. The first near Beacon Ida and the second in the general direction of the Happy Valley.'

Someone shouted:

'Thank God it's not the Ruhr tonight, anyway.'

'Window will be dropped, a bundle every ten minutes from the enemy coast. You will have 100 Squadron Defiants equipped with Mandrel[1] over the Channel in support. An Airborne Cigar[2]-equipped Lancaster will head the Main Force. You will also be pleased to hear that 54 Squadron Mosquitoes will be beating up Luftwaffe airstrips to keep the Nightfighters unhappy. If you have a problem on the return leg, remember that Darky and Sandra[3] are there to help you and that Manston and Fiskerton have FIDO[4] laid on if you run into ground fog.'

[1] A powerful airborne radio transmitter that broadcast intense noise interference on the exact frequency of Freya, part of the German radar system.

[2] An active jammer carried by special Lancasters to jam frequencies of the Luftwaffe ground control of interception.

[3] Guidance systems for returning planes.

[4] Fog Investigation Dispersal Operation.

Then it was the met officer's turn to give details of predicted cloud ceilings and formations, winds, and the possible hazards of icing and fog.

'The wind's shifting north, strength 5. It's blown up since this morning and there could be quite a heavy drift. If any clot tries hard enough, they might even end up in a Spanish gaol. There's an anticyclone centred over Silesia, but no cloud worth mentioning over the target. A Mosquito's out checking again now, so I'll keep you informed of any more changes at the final briefing.'

The signals officer then reeled off the frequencies of the night call-signs, and the latest information on German Nightfighter bands for the wireless operators to jam with Tinsel, a high-power transmitter broadcasting engine noise.

Finally it was time for the armaments officer to round things off. His message was short and to the point.

'No new toys. Four thousand-pound high-capacity cookies to blast out the windows and blast in the roofs. The rest of the load will be the usual 1400 four-pound thermite incendiaries.'

When it was over, Hunting and Maitland went to the next hut to check the flight plan again, with Collins tagging along behind them to draw his target map. Once they had unfolded their maps, Maitland sat down at the table and once more methodically worked out the course and track, based on the latest predicted wind-strengths. To stick to the planned course, the wind had to be allowed for, so that the actual track to be flown was adjusted for drift. There would be four course-changes on the legs going out, in theory at any rate. Kingston to Walcheren – three hundred and fifty miles; Walcheren to Koblenz – three hundred and twenty-five miles; Koblenz to the Friedberg marker – one hundred miles; Friedberg to the Emsdorf target indicators – ten miles. There were no specific plans for the return journey except to fly west by the shortest possible route. The minimum round-trip mileage would therefore be in the region of sixteen hundred miles.

While all this was going on, Collins asked:

'What's all this Mandrel and Airborne Cigar stuff and what's all this about Window?'

'Didn't they tell you? You should ask Eddie. He's the radio location king – they're mostly goon boxes to foul up Luftwaffe Nightfighter communications.'

Collins inspected the target map at a scale of four inches to the mile, revealing Emsdorf and the immediate countryside in the sinister night colours of black, white and mauve. The red target indicators would fall in a recreation ground in the northern suburb of Eschenheim.

For a moment Collins imagined himself alone in the Lancaster's nose with Emsdorf below and driblets of glycol defrosting the optical glass of his bombing window as he took P for Peter in on the bombing run through the darkness. For the best results, the Lancaster would have to fly straight and level for two minutes, the flying time, in fact, from the yellow marker at Friedberg to the target indicators, while the Mark XIV computer calculated drift and air-speed. Since P for Peter would be in the first wave, he would be bombing just behind the target indicators. He tried to imagine what the flak and the searchlights would be like, but couldn't, and then suddenly he didn't want to think about it any more. Then he realized that Hunting was looking at him.

'Are we going to be all right?'

'Of course we are, Sergeant, so long as the rear-gunner doesn't jinx us with his girl friend. I have every intention of coming through this one. All we'll have to do is take a grip and not do anything ropey.'

'None of us will have to do that.'

'Yeah, we perform well as a team.'

'After all, there has to be a first time and plenty of the others have got through.'

Maitland was now painfully working out a vertical section of the estimated track, even though every pilot in Bomber Command knew that the Ardennes rose no higher than fifteen hundred feet above sea-level.

'You'll have to stick to two thousand minimum to keep clear of trouble.'

'You don't have to tell me that, Professor.'

'It gets more interesting nearer the target. There are one or two hills touching three thousand in the Taunus.'

'Don't worry. I'll keep to 20,000 plus all the way, higher if the superchargers will let me.'

One of the advantages of the Lancaster over the Stirling and Halifax was the ceiling, which kept it out of range of medium flak and also made it a less vulnerable target for Nightfighters.

'Where was our rear-gunner?' Collins asked.

'Search me. It's a good job that all a straight A.G. has to worry about are his guns and a daily issue of Crooke's Halibut Liver Oil capsules.'

Bowls of these were put out at mealtimes in the Ops Mess to increase night vision.

'I don't suppose we'd even miss him if he got grounded.'

'I know I certainly would,' said Maitland, still deep in his calculations, without looking up.

'Why don't you try the NAAFI?' Hunting asked.

Sergeant Barton had not put in an appearance at the briefing because he was waiting for Sergeant Nicholls. He wanted to reassure her that he took no notice of the reputation that rumour had built up for her. In this way he wished to demonstrate that he cared for how she felt.

When she came in, she looked as pretty as ever, in spite of the severity of her uniform, which, in fact, far from detracting from her femininity, seemed to Barton to set it off. The fact of the matter was that Barton was lonely, feeling faintly homesick for the first time since he had left Australia. Although he was one of the crew, he did not feel part of it, not yet, not until they had been through an operation together and he had got the true measure of the other crew members, not to say himself. In the meantime, since he was a warm man, he wanted to be able to relate to somebody and feel close to them. And, it goes without saying, Sergeant Nicholls was a very attractive girl.

She bought a cup of tea and a cream slice and came over quite naturally to where he was sitting.

'When I saw you'd turned up, I knew that you couldn't have heard.'

'Heard what?'

'I'm not supposed to be a very lucky girl to know.'

Barton offered her a Players and lit it. She did not leave a lipstick mark on the untipped cigarette because she wasn't wearing any. Besides, she was not that sort of girl.

'Sometimes it really gets me down. I've applied for a posting more than once but nobody seems to listen. They seem to want me where I am. At least, the posting's never come through. It seemed the only decent thing after last time.'

'Let's hope it never does.'

'I knew them all. I sort of became a crew symbol. I used to do a lot of things for them, look after them, get them extra sandwiches on ops, but never tuck them up in bed at night, if you know what I mean.'

'You're all right.'

'You don't know what it can be like; and everyone's so nice about it. The permanent staff are always especially polite, as though I'm suffering from some incurable disease. Sort of solemn and sympathetic.'

'That's not the way I feel.'

'Oh well, I've tried to warn you off, but I see it isn't any use. I've been temporarily attached to five crews and all of them have bought it. There's a limit to the sort of emotional strain that kind of thing induces. I don't think I have feelings any more, or at any rate I've put them in cold storage for the duration. The only reason I came out for a drink with you was to boost my morale and prove to the Waafery girls that I wasn't totally leprous. Even then I could feel that they disapproved.'

'Were any of the crews that bought it Aussies?'

'Not to my knowledge.'

'Then in my case all this is rubbishing talk. There is no jinx.'

She said:

'You've no idea how much I appreciate your saying that.'

Barton said:

'Anyway, what did you do before all this?'

'I've done an awful lot of talking. Do you really want to know?'

'I'm a good listener.'

'I had to leave my grammar school early because Dad couldn't afford the fees. He was never very much good at money.'

'What did he do?'

'He was supposed to be a vet near Scarborough and that didn't help because it wasn't exactly a profitable practice, especially with the slump, and you had to get in with all the big farm managers, which Dad wasn't very good at either.'

She paused before going on.

'In the end we had to sell up and I had to get a job in Woolworths, the threepenny and sixpenny store. It was supposed to be a big come-down but I never noticed. I was thankful to get a job at all. The hours were ghastly, but I ended up as assistant manager.'

'Sounds like you did all right then.'

'There's nothing like a failure in the family to stimulate success. That's why this business about being nominated chop girl is so awful. I've no intention of being a failure myself.'

'It's clear you're not.'

'Anyway, there was an awful fuss when I got called up. Neither of them wanted me to leave home. But there were no two ways about it, and now I don't suppose I'll ever go back.'

'I know what you mean. I sometimes wonder whether Australia's right for me.'

'I thought it was a wonderful country.'

'The climate grows on you.'

For a moment Barton thought of the quiet routine boredom of the chartered accountants' firm in Sydney; tinned Christmas pudding at ninety degrees in the shade; the carefully graded rows of surburban houses and the never-ending preoccupation with home and Empire.

'You were saying that you left home.'

'That's right. When I was a WAAF, I knew I was doing something worth while and I didn't have to apologize for anything. I was accepted on my performance. The rest of the girls on my intake were grand, even though we were a mixed bag and one had to be terribly broad-minded.'

'I've never been overfond of tight little groups myself.'

'Some of us had never been away from home and some of us had had jobs. But once we were WAAFs, we had to do everything for ourselves. Nobody else would do it for us. On the other hand there was nobody else to get in the way.'

She paused for a moment and smiled.

'At my first operational posting there was this recreation room, totally cheerless and without even a single picture. Someone was an artist, someone else wangled brushes and paint and we all did murals right across it. It really looked bang on. We're all treated like responsible people, and I'm sure that things will be very different for girls after the war.'

'Roll on demob and out into civvy street.'

'You don't sound too keen.'

'Keen enough to get back in one piece.'

Outside the NAAFI they passed the camouflaged phone box, now padlocked and chained. There would be a full security flap inside the station until the last Lancaster returned from Emsdorf. Clixby Wolds was as cut off and isolated from the outside world as firmly as a town under siege. In the distance Barton could see that P for Peter was being bombed up.

'I'll be thinking of you,' Barton said. 'We must do this again.'

'I hope so too. I really do.'

They kissed on impulse in the shadows by the telephone exchange and then Sergeant Nicholls straightened her cap and said:

'Goodbye, Sergeant, and take care. I'll wave you off and

wave you in, you'll see.'

Collins came back to where Hunting was still painstakingly checking over Maitland's calculations step by step and inch by inch over Holland, Belgium and Germany.

'He isn't there.'

'Who isn't where?'

'Sergeant Barton. He wasn't in the NAAFI.'

'Then it probably means he didn't meet that girl, if it makes you feel any better. He's probably in the Ops Mess whacking into bacon and eggs. I suggest we forget about it and go and do the same thing.'

Collins felt that it was somehow improper of Barton to have missed the briefing, but on second thoughts it really didn't seem so important. At worst it showed an alarming degree of independence and a lack of the team spirit he had always taken for granted as being fundamental. In the end he put it down to the fact that Barton was an Australian.

6

Hänsel & Gretel

The Luftwaffe field at Hainaut in South Belgium hardly amounted to anything more than that. Set in the industrial countryside, it consisted of a tarmacked criss-cross, surrounded by makeshift sheds where the Me Bf-110Gs could be serviced under cover. There were, of course, also administrative huts and a dug-out armoury where ammunition and flares were stored, but by this time the Luftwaffe groundcrews were totally adapted to improvisation where and when the occasion demanded, having learned the hard way as the Geschwader leap-frogged forward behind the ever advancing front of the victorious Wehrmacht.

Although Hainaut had had time to put down roots since

it was overrun in the summer of 1940, it still retained a transitory, battle-tense feeling, as though the front line was still only a few kilometres away and they would have to be on the move tomorrow.

Krasnatsky welcomed this, since he did not care very much what conditions were like on any station and, being a true professional, he was only concerned with the job in hand. In a way, the worse conditions were, the better he liked it, since they were more than likely to escape the unwelcome attentions of the air staff.

The fact that they were north of the Meuse meant that, although the station was surrounded by farmland, the landscape was also dotted by derelict and working coal-pits. The consequent unaesthetic desolation of slag heaps, utilitarian red-brick engine houses and the reciprocating wheels of mine-shaft cages meant that it held little attraction for uniformed bureaucrats to drop in to lunch.

This also meant that the pilots of III/181 Staffel tended to be a tight little group keeping themselves to themselves. There were usually only ten pilots with an average of eight Nightfighters operational. These were, for the most part, veterans of the shooting-gallery war in Russia, although a few had also been involved in the earlier incursions into Poland, France and the Balkans. These experiences had made them old before their time in one way, but left them still as immature as schoolboys in others.

Perhaps Krasnatsky was slightly different because he was an old man at twenty-seven and he had remained a perfectionist. He did not want to do anything more in life than fight, which was why he had avoided being posted to a training unit as an instructor. In fact he was not very popular on the station in spite of his professional reputation, and his only close friend was the young Bavarian, Fritz Lange.

This friendship was really based on the working relationship that had developed between them as they pioneered their own variety of Nightfighter tactics, with Krasnatsky constantly polishing their tactical technique and finding out which was the best of the many new RD devices out of those he managed to borrow from the Technical Signals Units.

They worked so well together as a team it sometimes seemed that they were almost telepathic. One of Krasnatsky's favourite manoeuvres was to put in Lange as a decoy, and when the crew of the chosen bomber was distracted by Lange's first investigatory pass or flak flares, the Major would creep up to where he could administer a sudden *coup de grâce*. Lange was also useful in other ways; for example, if they lost the RD contact on their Lichtenstein radar, with its narrow twenty-five degree arc beam, they could divide the sky between them as they continued the search.

It could be said that much of Krasnatsky's success was due to Lange, even though he was the senior and more experienced pilot. Lange was quiet, passive, but determined, particularly when he had decided to press home an attack. But they were close enough to know that they really shared in each other's success and that the Major's Knight's Cross was a public relations exercise to improve civilian morale.

Nevertheless, Lange had been so close to his target on two occasions that his own Me-110 had been seriously damaged when the bomber had exploded and he had been forced to quick-jettison the upper canopy and bale out.

As Krasnatsky drove across Hainaut field, he passed the eight operational Me-110s of the Staffel that were in the middle of being serviced. There was something predatory and insect-like about them which the Major admired. He knew that the RAF bomber crews referred to them as 'crickets' or 'snappers' and, looking at the proboscis with its five Lichtenstein and SN-2 radar aerials jutting forward of the twin 30-mm and 20-mm cannon packs, he could only congratulate them on the accuracy of their description. There was also something grasshopper-like in the smooth round nose that merged with the cockpit canopy, where the pilot and wireless operator/rear-gunner sat.

There was something of the stick-insect in the tapering, delicate fuselage that ran for 43 feet from the aerials to the twin-rudder empannage. There was something of the menace of the hornet in the square-tipped narrowing wings with their forward-projecting twin 1475hp Daimler-Benz engine pods.

Every night a cloud of the deadly insects would rise over Europe, zooming over the Low Countries on patrol at 250 mph with endurance of four to five hours with their auxiliary tanks, long enough to follow the returning bomber stream well over the North Sea.

Dappled white and grey, the crickets lay waiting for nightfall as the black-overalled Luftwaffe mechanics checked the fluid levels in the coolant tanks.

When Krasnatsky arrived in his Kübelwagen[1] outside the complex of huts that formed the administrative block, Lange was in the Signals Workshop, testing the new Flensburg homing RD the Major had recently borrowed from Florennes. Flensburg was designed to pick up the radar pulse from 'Monica', a British warning device carried by RAF bombers that gave warning of an impending attack from the rear.

As usual, Krasnatsky took in what was going on at a glance. As Lange crouched over the test bench, Gissler, the RD mechanic, adjusted the input circuit to pick up the Monica pulse that was being beamed across the landing strip from the disused hut in the clump of stunted beech trees half a mile away.

'How's it going, Fritz?'

'It'll be a good back-up to Lichtenstein and not so temperamental. The signal's perfect now.'

'Anything to keep the Fighter Controller off my back. Which are you putting it in?'

'Hänsel.'

'Even better. I won't have to rely on ground signals to pick up a target.'

Krasnatsky's Nightfighter had been code-named Hänsel and Lange's Me-110 Gretel to prevent any confusion during night attacks.

[1] Open cross-country car (usually without doors and running-boards).

'By the way, the Flensburg's been fine-tuned, so don't start throwing your aircraft all over the sky. Gissler's going to do the job right now.'

'Don't worry, I'll see it's handled as gently as a Mädchen's tits.'

Krasnatsky peered into the shadows and examined the pale-blue cross centred in the middle of the cathode ray tube.

Gissel explained:

'When you pick up that signal, you're home and dry. It means you're following in the track of your target. The vertical track will move left or right as the target changes direction. Similarly the horizontal line registers altitude.'

'Has Hogel been shown how to use it?'

'He's like a maestro in a piano warehouse.'

'Good. I like it. Any trouble with the Eagles? My port aileron needed attention.'

'The Stab seems quite happy after this morning's test-flight.'

'O.K. then. We can all relax for a bit and switch on the BBC Forces Programme for Workers' Playtime. Personally I shall watch the sun going down over America.'

Lange said:

'If I were you, I should catch up on your beauty sleep, Major. You're going to need it. There's a signals alert.'

Krasnatsky yawned ostentatiously.

'What? Another late night?'

'It's on the cards. The listening posts on Schouwen have been picking up RAF test signals from East Anglia all morning.'

'Good. Well, I'll see you later. I'll be in my quarters.'

Lange raised his eyebrows.

'You mean you won't be available. Geschwader's putting us on stand-by from twenty hundred. We've been assigned to Dormouse Box by the air controller.'

'I'll be back in time. Don't worry.' Krasnatsky giggled nervously. 'Be a good chap and book a reserve bowser just for us. I may want to come back to fill up.'

Krasnatsky had felt the restlessness welling up inside him from the moment he had heard there was likely to be an operation that night. He could control the fear he sometimes felt without difficulty, but never his restlessness. He never felt that death was a likely outcome on any operation. If it came, he felt sure it would be accidental: a lucky hit by a Halifax rear-gunner, a flak battery ignoring his Night-fighter flares, or a Quax on his first operation confusing him with a Mosquito.

The restlessness was always with him now as a constant undercurrent. He never bothered to analyse it in detail, but he realized that it had something to do with the hunt and the kill. The excitement that overwhelmed him in the closing moments of an attack were just as addictive as a sniff of cocaine.

Out of the antidotes that were available and which were least likely to impair his performance he preferred sex. Alcohol certainly did not provide any kind of a solution.

Now he never needed Pervitin tablets to keep him awake, however long he flew. Quite the reverse. If he had ever felt the need to visit the medical officer, it would have been for a prescription for sleeping tablets.

Krasnatsky climbed into his Kübelwagen and tooted the horn for his driver.

'You can stand down, Marcks. I'll be back in time for take-off.'

'Yes, Herr Major.'

'Just see that my flying kit's laid out and waiting, and fix my thermos and sandwiches. After you've done all that, you can buzz off and give your mam'zelle a thrill. That's where I'm heading.'

The Comtesse Brigitte de Leguillac had been forced to settle in Brabant incognito, since it was safer for her to emigrate north to Belgium than to stay in her family house south of Périgueux, ever since her husband had vanished after unwisely expressing his disapproval of the Vichy régime. The transition had proved not too difficult in practical terms, since the de Leguillacs also owned a hunting lodge between Bastogne and St Hubert that had originally been a grant by Louis XIV. Now that she lived there, she occupied the time as a Luftwaffe auxiliary helper in Liège, which is how Krasnatsky had first met her.

The Major could not be sure whether Brigitte would be in or whether she was on duty, since she was not on the phone. In any event, it was immaterial, since, even if she was not there, his restless mood would be absorbed to some extent by the fifty-mile drive.

Krasnatsky tore through the wooded valleys of the Ardennes until he came to the familiar country track that led to the hunting lodge. Once he had asked Brigitte why she chose to live alone in such a place.

'That's easy. Having been brought up in the country, solitude doesn't bother me. In any case, it's best I keep my head down as things are.'

Krasnatsky smelled the sweet acrid scent of woodsmoke as his Kübelwagen bumped along the track; Brigitte was burning last winter's beech leaves. The de Leguillacs had carefully nurtured chestnuts, oaks and beeches among the surrounding pines. The Comtesse was wearing slacks and a blouse that set her figure off well, although clearly she didn't need to pay much attention to how she dressed. She showed no surprise at his arrival, as though it was perfectly natural for him to be there.

The Comtesse straightened up and narrowed her eyes against the golden afternoon sun as Krasnatsky switched off the noisy engine.

'You know, I had a feeling you might come.'

Krasnatsky kissed her hand.

'You know me, Comtesse, restless, unpredictable, always hand in hand with the unexpected.'

'You look a little tired to me. You'd better come inside and have a brandy.'

'Comtesse, I like that idea. That is an idea I like. You

know I shall be flying tonight?'

'Oh, you will, will you? Then I can guess what this visit means.'

She turned and opened the door, the sunlight catching her fine-boned face. Krasnatsky had known that she was an aristocrat from the moment he first saw her. That finely moulded nose below a high forehead and that delicately proportioned mouth. Just like the face of one of the caryatids he remembered from the Acropolis, that hot August in Athens in 1941, before he and Lange went on Nightfighters.

There was no doubt about it, Brigitte was quite superb. To measure her against the two little tarts from the Brussels red-light hotel was like comparing a Lancaster with a couple of clapped-out Bolshevik Tupolev TB-3s.

Inside, the room was panelled in dark oak and carried hunting trophies.

'I feel out of place here,' she said. 'It would suit you better with your sporting instincts.'

'It's the kind of place one would take one's mistress.'

'Yes, it's the kind of place you deserve.'

The Comtesse spoke with a hint of bitterness, although she was really quite fond of Major Krasnatsky.

'Why pick on me? I'm a practising Social Democrat, not some Junker squire who insists that everyone should address him as Graf. Hadn't you noticed? They've abolished class distinction in the Third Reich.'

'That's a laugh,' said the Comtesse, taking a bottle of Grande Champagne Segonzac off the shelf of the oak corner cupboard.

'Anyway, you'll always be a hunter, however you choose to think of yourself. The Ardennes is full of legends about hunters. St Hubert down the road is named after their patron saint.'

'I wouldn't know about that. Churches bore me. It must be something to do with the life I lead.'

'What kind of life is that?'

'On permanent stand-by. God knows what'll happen when it's all over.'

'On permanent stand-by?'

Krasnatsky giggled and brushed his fingertips across his eyepatch.

'That's the reason I'm here now, Comtesse.' He gave a child's imitation of a machine-gun burst. 'Shoot you down in flames. Total victory.'

The Comtesse sighed, her large dark eyes weighing him up like a mother deciding how large a slice of cake her naughty child deserved. Then she laughed.

'I don't know where you find the energy to keep up your obsession.'

'I've come to the conclusion,' Krasnatsky said, after taking a sip of brandy, 'that it's something to do with being reared in a Prussian bog. For one thing, nothing really grows along the Baltic except swamp grass and rye, so you have the perfect opportunity for seeing nature uncamouflaged. Everything's hunting everything else. That is, until the wind blows from the steppes, and then it's too freezing to do anything except make love. That's not too easy considering the distinct lack of elegant ladies, which is why I find you such agreeable company.'

'Well, this isn't exactly an East Prussian farmhouse.'

'A hundred times more civilized.'

The Comtesse sat down on the dark carved chair in front of the fire and hunched her shoulders as though she found it chilly.

'You're not bad for a womanizer.'

'Half the trouble is that I really like women. It's just that I never find time to get to know them. Anyway, having that kind of reputation makes one unpopular in the mess – it makes some people jealous.'

Brigitte reached out and placed two apple logs on the fire and they began to fill the room with their subtle woodland sweetness.

'You're probably exaggerating. It's probably the Knight's Cross that they envy.'

Krasnatsky giggled again:

'It should really be the Lady's Cross.'

For a moment the Major held her gently and kissed

her behind the ear.

'Even though I am just a Prussian, I try and do everything artistically even if it's disposing of a four-engined heavy.'

They lay against each other for a moment in the firelight on the faded Bokhara carpet.

'What do you want exactly?' the Comtesse asked as she dipped her finger in the brandy glass and flicked the droplets onto the logs so that they flared and sizzled momentarily.

'I want to relax.'

'That's a lot to ask considering the state of both our lives.'

Krasnatsky ignored the remark as he began to unbutton the Comtesse. As he did so, he remembered that the girl called Emmeline had started to cry when he offered both of them money. Although it was a compliment, he had broken the golden rule that was to treat tarts like comtesses and comtesses like tarts.

He felt Brigitte's heavy breasts brush lightly against his chest with nipples erect. She opened her eyes.

'D'you know something? I get so bored. I ask you, me bored, in the middle of a World War.'

'I'll fuck you here. It'll be easier that way.'

'That'll be divine.'

As he entered her, Brigitte moved her lips, with eyes tight shut, as though conversing in a secret and silent language. Her whole body lay relaxed against the antique couch except for her thighs, where she gripped Krasnatsky so tightly he found it almost too painful to make love.

As this constriction and the sympathy that they felt together began to produce a simultaneous release, Krasnatsky suddenly found himself mentally in a hypnagogic Never-Never-Land, projected through the war-torn night sky, above the winking morse of fighter beacons and wavering searchlight beams, below a roof of exploding flak. Hurtling through a dim grey corridor of nothing towards the flaring exhausts of a giant bomber inexorably passing on its bomb-run.

When he opened his eyes, he found that the Comtesse was searching his face. She gave him a kiss.

'You saw something. What was it you saw? I sometimes see things too when it happens.'

Krasnatsky giggled to conceal the fact he wasn't in the mood to answer questions. Maybe he should try and get some leave when things like that started to happen.

'Can't you guess, Comtesse? The hunt, the hunt. Now I should appreciate two of your best black-market eggs and a slice of genuine Ardennes cured ham. I'm going to be kept pretty busy tonight.'

Without saying another word, Brigitte obediently got up and, hitching a black leather coat across her shoulders, lit a candle from the glowing embers of the fire. Then she went to the kitchen.

Krasnatsky had another glass of brandy and then got dressed, irritated to find that his mind returned time after time to St Hubert, rather in the same way that a crossword devotee worries about an elusive clue.

'Who was this St Hubert anyway?' he suddenly called. 'Why are hunters supposed to like him so much? What made him so wonderful?'

'It's nothing really. He just went hunting on Good Friday and met up with an eloquent stag with a cross between its antlers. It warned him to mend his ways or he would burn for ever in hell. It was an instant conversion and shortly afterwards they made him a bishop.'

'Sounds as though he didn't have much choice.'

'Probably Church propaganda to ensure that people ate fish on Fridays.'

'Well, at least he got his promotion, besides being mentioned in dispatches.'

Krasnatsky suddenly had a mental picture of the cruciform shape of the last Stirling he had shot down, back-lit starkly against the raging seas of fire below.

Brigitte sensed that she could not get through to him in his present mood and put it down to the suppressed strain of his one hundred and three confirmed victories against bombers. Tonight it could go up to four or five and then he would be round to her again, restless, restless as he waited for the next climax of love or destruction.

'That's much better,' Krasnatsky said, pushing away his plate. 'Thank you for everything. You've set me up for the night besides giving me food for thought.'

'Don't even think about it. Drop in whenever you feel inclined. There'll always be some kind of a welcome. As I told you, boredom seems to be my kind of problem.'

Brigitte cried for twenty minutes after the roar of the Kübelwagen was lost in the empty forest, although it was for no reason. She only hoped she would see him again one day.

7

Dispersals

The crew of P for Peter stood outside Briefing in the late golden light waiting for the grey Bedford three-tonner that sometime was going to take them to the Lancaster standing ready at the far corner of Dispersals.

They felt clumsy in their flying clothes and looked it. Since the distance to the nearest aircraft was at least half a mile, they would be taken there by truck to avoid the sweating that even a leisurely walk would entail. This could have disastrous results above 13,000 feet and might result in frostbite. The maximum Lancaster ceiling was four thousand feet higher than the Alps.

They waited impassively in silence, listening restlessly to the sounds of elation coming from the Ops Mess, where Z for Zebra's crew were busy celebrating the fact that their operation looked like being scrubbed, since on pre-flight a fault had been belatedly discovered in the hydraulic compressor, with the result that the bomb-bay doors remained open and the flaps firmly down. Z for Zebra had been the first aircraft scheduled for take-off and, unless the fault could be corrected in the next thirty minutes to let them tag onto the end of the bomber stream, they might never take off that night at all.

They had started to sing intermittently, partly at the prospect of a possible reprieve and partly to release nervous tension. The sounds coming through the open windows of the Ops Mess indicated that the prospect of being non-runners did not depress them unduly:

'Cats on the rooftops, cats on the tiles,
Cats with syphilis, cats with piles,
Cats with their arseholes wreathed in smiles
As they revel in the joys of copulation.'

The crew of P for Peter still stood silently, although each of them was straining his ears to hear what would happen next. They stood motionless, clustered round their valises and parachute packs like a Victorian family off to the seaside. Only Collins looked mildly disapproving.

Then another voice interrupted:

'I say, Brian, cut out the blue stuff, will you? You'll have the WAAF Orderly Dog down all our necks. And don't start up *Mussolini's Organ Grinders* either.'

There was a pause and Barton shifted his position restlessly. Then the piano inside the Mess crashed into the opening bars of *My Darling Clementine*. The crew of Z for Zebra caught up the tune and began to roar out:

At the beacon, at the beacon,
Landing turn is number nine,
And the aircraft are all saying:
'One more turn and I've had mine.'

Comes a fighter, comes a fighter,
Comes a Junkers eighty-eight.
Hurry, Archie. Hurry, Archie
Or you'll be too fucking late.

Hello, Darky. Hello, Darky.
There's a fighter giving chase.
Hello, Darky. Hello Darky.
What the hell's the course for base?

Hello, aircraft. Hello, aircraft.
What's it got to do with me?
Circle beacon. Circle beacon.
QFE is nine two three.

The breeze ruffled the light-blue flag with its red, white and blue roundel that stood to one side of the tarmacked parade-ground as the voices continued:

Hello, Darky. Hello, Darky.
Aircraft's shooting hard at me.
Hello, aircraft. Hello, aircraft.
Shoot it down, says PAD.

Hello, Darky. Hello, Darky.
We've received and understood.
Remove fingers, remove fingers.
Bastard's down in Crapper's Wood.

Hello, Darky. Hello, Darky.
Can I come in now and land?
Hello, aircraft. Hello, aircraft.
Do you want the bleeding band?

A grey three-tonner came into sight halfway from Dispersals, the canvas canopy flapping.

Hello, aircraft. Hello, aircraft.
Get a green when you are near.
Hello, Archie. Hello, Archie.
I have left the flare-path clear.

Now that the three-tonner was only one hundred yards away, they could see that it was being driven by a WAAF.

To the Ops Room, to the Ops Room
From Dispersal we must go.
What the fuck's gone wrong with transport?
Christ Almighty, aren't they slow!

The truck stopped in front of them, the chains rattling against the tail-board that swung at the back of the chassis. They started to pile on the parachutes and holdalls.

> We are down, sir. We are down, sir.
> And no thanks to Sentinel 2.
> Our results, sir, thanks to Met, sir,
> Our results we leave to you.

The silence, now that the WAAF driver had switched off the engine, coincided with the end of the singing as they heard through the Mess window:

'Is it safe to sink another pint, Skip?'

Someone else answered:

'Not to worry, Chopper, that kite's well and truly grounded. The gremlins are always tough to winkle out, once they're bedded down in compressed air. O.K., boys, this round's on me.'

There was a burst of cheering.

The crew of P for Peter climbed on board without further comment, the memory of the singing leaving them thoughtful and mildly subdued, as though they were part of a funeral cortège that had been overtaken by a wedding. Then Hunting, hanging onto the canopy support, said:

'O.K., boys, let's snap out of it. The laugh will be on them once we get back with an op chalked up and another one for them to do.'

'Who were those sods anyway?' Howells asked as the three-tonner bumped off.

'Z for Zebra, twenty-three ops,' Collins said.

'Christ, almost a full tour.'

'Our officer's a gen kiddie,' said Barton. 'Got all the answers, the lovely man.'

'They're mad to be happy about it,' said Fairclough. 'By all accounts Emsdorf should be a piece of cake. It's only a hundred miles inside.'

'Inside where?' Barton asked.

'Don't worry, cobber, you'll soon find out where.'

The WAAF driver changed down jerkily as she turned

the truck onto the hard standing beside P for Peter. When they got out, Hunting noticed that Collins was holding a battered teddy-bear. Collins said defensively:

'Just a silly idea. We got acquainted at Training Unit and it seems a suitable moment for "Bossy" to join the crew. He's going to look after the Mark XIV computer with me and scare away the snappers.'

Hunting said:

'Nice meeting you, Bossy. Welcome on board.'

Then he solemnly shook hands with the teddy-bear as the Chiefie came up holding the clip-board with the RAF 700.

'All the bugs sorted out, Sergeant. RT, the lot.'

Hunting glanced over at Howells, the flight engineer, who nodded and put up a thumb.

'Seemed fine to me.'

'O.K. then, let's get cracking,' Hunting said.

After starting up and with the chocks jammed tightly in position against the treadless balloon tyres, Hunting moved the throttles forward until the four revolution-counters in front of him registered full revs on each engine and the props became invisible revolving scythes, as P for Peter vibrated and shuddered against the full power of the four Merlins.

Hunting said against the scream of the engines:

'O.K. Pre-flight everybody. Ready, Howells?'

Howells began the formal catechism of checks as Hunting's fingers moved over the control panel, constantly checking and rechecking the instruments and switches, while the other crew members waited restlessly at their stations for the moment of take-off.

'Pressures and temperatures.'

'All O.K.'

'Hydraulics.'

'Flaps down ... up and indicating.'

'Bomb doors.'

'Closed.'

'Booster pumps.'

'Off.'

'Rad shutters.'
'Open.'
'Magnetos.'
'All checked and serviceable.'
Hunting eased back the throttles, and the wail and scream of the protesting props were reduced to a growling, impatient roar.
'O.K. Ending run-up checks,' said Hunting. 'Call the pre-taxi checks, Engineer.'
'Ground/flight switch.'
'On flight.'
'Nav lights.'
'On.'
'Altimeter.'
'QFE is set.'
'Instruments.'
'All serviceable.'
'Suction.'
'4½.'
'Rad shutters.'
'Open.'
'Brakes.'
'Pressures O.K.'
'Pre-taxi check completed,' said Hunting. 'O.K., Sergeant Howells, we're ready to roll.'
Howells gave the thumbs-up sign through the open window and the ground-crew pulled away the chocks.
After waiting three minutes for the green, Hunting taxied out on all four engines, turning from P for Peter's dispersal area onto the perimeter track by giving first the port outer and then the starboard outer a burst of throttle, constantly keeping his hand on the brake to prevent the Lancaster from surging forward.
There were no aircraft following them up the perimeter track and none in front. They were last in the queue and the fitters were still working on the hydraulic system of Z for Zebra.
Hunting took P for Peter up to the beginning of the runway and brought the Lancaster to a halt.

'Right, Engineer. Final pre-take-off check.'
Someone said over the intercom:
'About time too. Much more of this and I'll go spare.'
Howells started to intone monotonously:
'Autopilot.'
'Clutch in, cock out.'
'DR compass.'
'Set and operating.'
'Pitot heater.'
'On.'
'Trimmer.'
'Elevator Two forward, others to neutral.'
'Pitch.'
'Fully fine.'
'Fuel.'
'Contents checked. Master cocks on. Number two tanks selected. Crossfeeds off. Booster pumps on.'
'Superchargers.'
'M Gear.'
'Air intake.'
'Cold.'
'Rad shutters.'
'On auto.'
'Flaps.'
'Set to take-off and indicating.'
'Final pre-flight take-off check completed,' Hunting said slowly, glancing carefully over the control panel.
'The Watch Office has given you a green,' Howells said.

Trapper McIndoe, seated in the grandstand of the rear upper turret, also saw the Aldis winking green from the black-and-white chequered caravan beside them as the heavily laden Lancaster wallowed forward along the runway and slowly gathered speed.
A line of permanent staff and ground-crew were ahead of them towards the end of the runway, but standing well back. Some of them were saluting and others had raised their

arms in Churchill's V for Victory. McIndoe caught the chevrons of a WAAF sergeant at the end of the line. She was not wearing a cap and he noticed how the evening sun brought out the highlights of her fair hair.

Then he concentrated on take-off, willing the heavy Lancaster forward and off the ground. It was a moment that he particularly disliked, only too well aware that he was riding slightly aft of thirteen tons of petrol and high explosive and that something unexpected like a burst tyre could blow them all to kingdom come.

Take-off was extremely important to Trapper McIndoe since he regarded it as one of the greatest operational hazards because he had no control. Once they were unstuck and a thousand feet up, he would feel much safer.

Then, as the waving line of RAF personnel flashed by, he rocked in his seat again to will the aircraft up as it finally reached the speed of no return. For a bleak moment he thought that Hunting was going to run out of runway as they came towards the first of the red warning lamps, but then he felt the tail ease up, and a few seconds later P for Peter clawed into the sky, the four Merlins throatily fighting the pull of gravity, the nose uneasily poised to a flat thirty-degree angle as the thirty-two tons of aircraft slowly rose away from Clixby Wolds.

Over the intercom he heard Hunting say:

'Brakes on – brakes off. Undercarriage up. 2850 revs and plus 6 boost.'

McIndoe was flooded with a sense of relief as the undercarriage bumped into the inner nacelles and there was an appreciable increase in air-speed.

'O.K. Climbing out now.'

The Lancaster's port wing dipped as it slowly soared up across the T24 hangars, huts and Watch Office to the south of the elongated oval of the perimeter track linking the main runway to the empty dispersal points now deserted except for the immobile silhouette of Z for Zebra.

The intercom crackled again:

'Undercarriage up. Lights out. Safety speed. Flaps up. 2650 and plus 4.'

After the tension of take-off a feeling of anti-climax now settled over P for Peter's crew as the Lancaster slowly circled westwards on a long ellipse, the apogee of which was Liverpool, and they steadily gained height.

The countryside below was dark and neutral and seemingly lifeless, and yet almost every able-bodied man and woman was working in the country or cities to shorten the life of Hitler's Germany.

On the return leg over Birmingham they reached the cloud base at fifteen thousand feet and, as the outside temperature dropped away, Hunting listened for the clatter of ice from the port air-screws, as the props flung it against the fuselage skin. He worked the windscreen de-icing pump fixed to the right-hand corner of his seat, and the glycol misted over the windscreen. The dying sun occasionally broke through the interlaced cloud segments and, in spite of the cabin heater, frost formed glittering stars on the window panels and astrodome.

The damper round the starboard inner exhaust flared momentarily and Hunting saw the opaque glaze of rime that now ran across the wing, dulling the dark-green and earth-brown of the topside camouflage.

The crew had passed the long, time-consuming circuit over England in various states of boredom. Hunting was, of course, fully occupied in flying the Lancaster, as was Howells in monitoring his engineer's panel. Maitland busied himself in taking fixes and calling off the correctional bearings to change their course.

Collins occupied the time by flicking over the pages of 'Razzle' and 'London Opinion' in the forward solitude of the air bomber's compartment. Fairclough tried to gauge the likely reactions of the other crew members, deciding that Maitland was inclined to be fussy and therefore unpredictable in unforeseen situations. Barton scanned the sky for enemy aircraft, although common sense told him that there would be no intruders at that altitude over England. A Heinkel sneaking in low over the North Sea to try its luck, maybe, but nothing more than that.

McIndoe, however, was absorbed in his private obsession with escape. When they had drawn chutes, he had been particularly careful to take up the ration boxes that were available. These took the form of a water bottle whose side unscrewed to reveal a magnetized button; a map of Europe printed on silk; two dozen packets of Horlicks tablets; and a dozen OXO cubes.

Earlier he had been careful to acquire the flying boots from which the leather uppers could be ripped to leave what looked like a perfectly normal pair of civilian shoes.

He also concealed about him other useful aids: some French francs, a steel mirror and razor, a fishing line and hooks. It was his opinion that, if the worst should happen, all he had to do after baling out would be to make his way to France or Belgium, where his troubles would be more or less over, since he could speak French fluently and he did not think that many Germans would be able to detect his Canadian accent.

The problem of baling out was not, however, entirely straightforward and he had gone into it in some detail.

This was because the official exit was the hatch in the floor of the air bomber's compartment in the nose. In an emergency it would probably take four minutes for him to reach it, encumbered by his electrically heated suit and his chute. This, in his view, was three minutes too long.

He had calculated that he would have a much better chance of getting out at the rear entry door just at the back of his station. However, two things had to be taken into account to achieve this: the position of the aircraft and the door itself.

So far as the first was concerned, if the aircraft was nose-down and diving, he would fall clear of the tail plane, but if the Lancaster was flying straight and level, or nose-up, there would be some risk of his body striking the tail-plane spar or rudder, which could result, at best, in a broken arm or leg.

On the other hand, if the aircraft was flying straight and level, this would mean that the emergency was not critical, and there should be plenty of time for him to go forward and take his turn with the others at the air bomber's hatch.

So far as the rear door was concerned, since the hinges were on the right and it opened outwards, he would have to use the axe from the fuselage wall to sever it from the airframe. It was a calculated risk, but preferable to the length of time it could take McIndoe to wriggle out with his parachute through the turret port and negotiate the main spar steps forward, before making his way along the narrow corridor to starboard and down past the pilot into the air bomber's compartment.

At 10,000 feet Hunting said:

'Oxygen on, please, Eddie.'

The wireless operator was stationed close to the oxygen control valve. Thirty seconds later, oxygen began to hiss through his economizer and simultaneously Hunting felt the gentle, steady stream within his mask.

'Yarmouth in fifteen minutes, Cap.'

Now they were above the cloud and soon they would be leaving behind them the familiar, precarious security of wartime England as they passed the rendezvous point and joined the bomber stream, twenty thousand feet over Yarmouth. It would take them about the same time to fly to Germany as it had done to circuit the Midlands.

As P for Peter reached the 20,000 foot ceiling which the Main Force first wave had been allocated, Hunting, flying into the darkening eastern sky, thought how appropriate it was that night should fall first over Europe. On the far right he still caught glimpses of the setting sun as it splashed the streaks of towering cumulus behind them with purple and gold.

Hunting checked his watch and saw that they were dead on schedule as Maitland said over the intercom:

'Time to set course, Cap. Zero niner fife, magnetic.'

It was only then that Hunting realized the last aircraft

they had seen was Z for Zebra. Now they were well and truly on their own.

The Met had given them three-tenths cloud over Europe as far as the Rhine, with broken four-tenths over the target. The cloud base ranged from twelve thousand to eighteen thousand feet along their course. Although it would provide some cover, this would be balanced by the danger from icing.

Hunting took in the broad band of instruments, noting that the revolutions on each of the indicator dials hovered at 2650. All, that is, except the starboard inner which wavered at a hundred revolutions below. Hunting tapped Howells on the shoulder and pointed, and the flight engineer nodded against the roar of the engines, before turning to his panel to pull the booster switch.

Far below them lay the sea and it was becoming darker minute by minute.

Now they were entering the no-man's-land in front of Europe and, although they naturally assumed command of the air up to the Dutch coast, the Luftwaffe could always be present to challenge that assumption. The presence of the bomber stream had already been noted by tracking stations from Denmark to Le Havre and its direction plotted as it headed towards the main line of German radar-controlled Nightfighter defences that lay in a broad band across Europe, fifty miles inland, in Holland, Belgium and Northern France but turning further east in Southern France.

Apart from a flak ship, they could feel comparatively safe over the sea until they passed through the first belt of coastal defences with their flak and searchlight batteries controlled by short-range Ansbach and Nashorn radar that ran along the shoreline of Europe.

Hunting switched on the intercom.

'Gunners, better test the Brownings now.'

As the nose dipped, Hunting caught sight of Collins' helmeted head in the forward gun turret and twin parallels of tracer stabbed ahead towards Europe.

The gunners reported all guns working as Hunting

glanced right, over his shoulder, to where Howells was standing in front of his flight engineer's panel. Then he heard Howells say with an undertone of panic:

'The inner starboard's overheating. The oil temperature's rising.'

Hunting checked the RPM indicator and saw that the revolutions were falling. At the same time the Lancaster juddered as the Merlin backfired and coughed.

'What the hell is it?'

'The supercharger must be u/s. The fuel booster pump's at maximum and the coolant temperature's still rising.'

Hunting said:

'Shall I go down?'

Then he heard Barton say:

'That's great! Just as we're going to hit the Dutch coast.'

Howells said thinly:

'The only sensible thing to do is scrub and go back.'

Hunting said:

'We're not here because we're sensible.'

Howells' voice assumed a slightly nagging note:

'There's nothing sensible about a red-hot engine either.'

Hunting felt his stomach contract:

'What you're saying is that the inner starboard could burst into flames.'

'Yes, I am. Feather, switch off and turn back.'

Collins said:

'Too bad we've made it this far.'

The supercharger compensated for the drop in atmospheric density resulting from their altitude and the increasing rarity of the atmosphere some three miles above the earth's surface, by re-cycling the engine's exhaust fumes to drive a turbine forcing air into the cylinders. The air was drawn through a duct which also served the carburettors. This duct, mounted on the starboard side of the nacelle, was faced with an anti-ice guard which protected the air intake. The anti-ice guard had now partially failed, allowing ice to form inside the air intake duct. This gradually affected the air compression and, since the engine could no longer run smoothly, resulted in overheating as the Merlin strained to generate power on an inadequate ratio of oxygen to high octane fuel.

Barton said:

'Turning back at this stage is a ropey idea. There's Lancs and Stirlings as thick as fleas on a rabbit's bum from here back to Kingston on Hull. We're in the first wave, remember. Maybe the flight engineer likes the idea of driving against the traffic down a one-way street in the rush hour.'

Hunting knew that Barton was right. It would be madness to fly against the general flow of the bomber stream. The odds in favour of collision would be enormous.

'We could peel off and head south,' Howells suggested edgily.

Hunting said:

'We'd be crossing the width of the stream. No, I don't like that idea much either. Anyway, I'm going to feather.'

The sergeant pilot reached down to the pedestal and switched off the master fuel cock and then he held in the feathering button just long enough for it to stay in by itself. Seconds later, the button sprang back as the feathering was completed. This meant that the starboard inner propeller was now disengaged from the Merlin's crankshaft. Hunting then gradually closed the throttle. When the RPM indicator dropped to zero, he switched off the engine.

The consequence of this was a drop in air-speed from 160 to 125 miles an hour and the Lancaster began to lose height, although Hunting knew that he would be able to resume straight and level flight when the altimeter registered 10,000 feet.

However, cutting out the starboard inner Merlin closed down its generator, the front-turret hydraulic pump and the compressor operating the pneumatic system. P for Peter was in trouble.

Maitland asked anxiously:

'What air-speed are you making now, Cap?'

'130. I'm going to increase revolutions to make 140.'

Maitland came back after making a rapid calculation.

'Then you better alter course to a heading of 118.'

The navigator entered in his log:

'22.43 hrs. Engine failure on starboard inner, 107 miles on course from Yarmouth. Speed reduced to 130 mph.'

Now that the engine was feathered, Hunting was able to turn his attention to what to do next. A speed of 130 mph at 10,000 feet was much too slow for comfort when crossing the Dutch coast. The monstrous realities of the situation almost overwhelmed him as they flew towards the enemy flak belt, and yet the suggested alternatives seemed equally wrong. Behind them the bomber stream would be staggered in layers with the Stirlings at their maximum ceiling of just below 15,000 feet. P for Peter was solidly wedged under the invisible bomber stream now overtaking them overhead.

Collins said:

'Enemy coast coming up. I saw some lights.'

'Give me a rough fix, Professor.'

'It'll only be dead reckoning. We should cross between Knokke and Nieuwe Sluis.'

'What does the flak map say?'

'Seems O.K. So long as we steer clear of Ostend and Bruges.'

Ahead, Hunting could see a faint tracery of searchlights welcoming the bomber stream. To the crew of P for Peter it seemed that they were specially intended for them.

Fairclough said:

'Isn't there anything you can think of, Cap? When they spot our blip on their radar, they'll know we're a lame duck and give us the treatment.'

The sky ahead was now erupting in sudden fairy glows of light, broken lines of incandescent red and green that shot erratically across the black velvet sky and then were gone.

Collins said knowledgeably:

'Light flak.'

'We should be out of range.'

Searchlights began to swing their broad white diffusing beams this way and that. The light penetrated the aircraft, creating a sinister, luminous glow.

'Shouldn't we be shovelling out Window?' Fairclough asked.

'You better do that small thing.'

P for Peter suddenly shook and bucked as a line of exploding red blossoms appeared and vanished below.

'That's not bloody light flak.'

Now the flowers came back to blossom in regular geometrical rows, ahead and behind them, as though they were negotiating some sinister flare-path. The starboard wing rose and fell violently and the nacelles throbbed against the main spar. Hunting could see the metal skin rippling with the stress. He felt icy cold inside his Irvine jacket and gripped the control column as the bottom of the world fell away. The night ahead changed to a blinding light as more red flowers blossomed with a flash, revealing for a second a dangling foliage of smoke. This time there was the rattle of metal against metal, a scratching, grating sound as though something was lightly brushing the side of the fuselage.

Barton shouted:

'They got our bloody range, Cap. You better move it.'

Hunting eased forward the stick and took the Lancaster into a shallow dive.

Howells said nervously:

'For Christ's sake, how long d'you reckon we'll get away with this on three engines?'

'For as long as it takes to get to Emsdorf. Professor, try and get a fix on Gee.'

'I'll try, but there's a lot of jamming.'

As he dived, Hunting became all too aware of the thin increasing incandescence of the light flak that rose in a curtain to meet them. What he had done was to obey a gut reaction which might, quite possibly, turn out to be wrong. He felt, however, that Fairclough had a point and that they had already been picked out as a lame duck. At least the air-speed was creeping up, even on three engines, to a more healthy 160 mph, though the altimeter reading had fallen from 10 to 9 to 8000 feet.

'I'm going to try the dodgy engine again, Engineer. Stand by with the booster after a switch-on.'

'That's against Air Ministry Instructions. It's almost certain to start a fire. We're in enough trouble as it is.'

'Let's wait and see.'

The flak patterns began to fall behind them with their increase in speed, and Hunting could tell now that the barrage was reaching up above their heads.

The sergeant pilot eased out of the dive and held the Lancaster straight and level, compensating once more for the aircraft's tendency to yaw to port. Opening the throttle, he pushed down the propeller control and switched on the ignition. A flame shot out of the exhaust damper as he held in the feathering button, and the revolutions gradually climbed to 1500.

The engine was firing perfectly and Howells confirmed that the coolant and oil temperature-readings were normal. The loss in height had dissipated the ice which had formed inside the ice guard and the Merlin now ran as sweetly as it had done on the afternoon's test-flight. The Lancaster surged forward and Hunting began to weave, pushing up the revolutions until the air-speed indicator stood at 170 mph.

Then Hunting realized that they were through the flak and he could see no more lights and that they were once more in the shelter of the comforting darkness.

He said:

'O.K., everybody?'

Everyone answered except McIndoe, and so Hunting said to Fairclough:

'Take a break from jamming the Jerry radar and plug in McIndoe's intercom.'

'Roger, Cap.'

Hunting had tried to keep the sudden anxiety he felt out of his voice, while the rest of the crew waited, tense and expectant. They waited for what seemed an eternity for Fairclough to report back.

8

Brown Bear

From the nearby Wolfspitze, Luftkommando Operations Centre (West) stood out in the undulating landscape like some grotesque, giant Christmas cake, its one hundred and eighty foot square walls decorated with festoons of camouflage netting. On top of the sixty-foot-high bunker a carefully created pastoral scene had been arranged to disguise the fifteen-foot bomb-proof steel-and-concrete roof. There was even a hamlet complete with village church, on which the moon shone fitfully.

The core of this cake, as one would suppose, contained rather more than charms and silver groschen. Within was arranged a self-sufficient complex to service the III Luftflotte Signals Regiment, RAD operators, telephonists, telex and radio operators, with their ancillary servicing staff, besides the nucleus of Operations Control, who day by day and night by night allocated and directed the resources of the electronic Siegfried Line that stretched from the North Sea to Biscay.

The dark pine forests of the Eifel spread out in serried avenues surrounding Brown Bear, the forest rides carrying the thousands of cables that connected the Operations Centre to its most distant substations spread along the European coast.

From Oostvoorne in Southern Holland, the Heidelberg Early Warning Station probed 200 miles towards England, flanked by a long line of Freyas. Next lay the wide band of Himmelbett medium radars running in an irregular line from Denmark, through Belgium to the heart of France; code-named Tom Tit, Hamster, Butterfly, Wasp, Gorilla, Robin, Beaver and Dormouse with their complementary Nightfighter fields at St Dizier, Rheims, Champagne, Florennes, St Trond, Venlo, Gilze Rijen, Enschede, Staden and Hainaut.

The lines also extended to the control rooms of the flak batteries along the coastal defence belt and the subordinate areas surrounding the cities from the great kidney shape of the Ruhr industrial complex to the minor ellipses and circles of Amsterdam, Rotterdam, Antwerp, Brussels, Lille, Cambrai, Liège and Koblenz. The gunnery radar on these Ansbach and Nashorn sites also tracked the bomber stream for the flak and searchlight units.

The operations complex at the heart of Brown Bear was a catalyst for the emotions that flowed back from each one of these individual cells; and, as the least-evolved living organism withdraws instinctively from the menace of an invading foreign body, so these impulses of fear and expectation were transmitted to the centre, tempered by the exultation that can come from a sudden and unforeseen victory.

This feeling of terrible and tragic drama was confined each night in the Operations Theatre, where the proscenium arch was filled with a thirty-foot-square opaque glass plot of Denmark, Holland, Belgium, Northern France and, of course, Germany. The drama was being enacted by a permanent cast of forty-eight Luftwaffe girl auxiliaries who sat ranged in six steeply rising rows behind the screen, each with a light projector, whose beams combined to define the approach and direction of the bomber stream plotted from the incoming reports of the RAD controllers.

The audience faced them, hidden by the opacity of the screen, also ranged in a steep bank of five ascending stalls. The Royal box, at the top, was occupied by the Chief Operations Officer, his Broadcast Officer to his right, above the twenty-four Fighter Liaison Officers, who sat in direct contact with the Nightfighter airfields throughout Northwest Europe.

The hidden currents had been at work in the Operations Room ever since the first Heidelberg contact, confirmed by the medium-range Würzburg stations, had indicated the certainty of a bomber attack that night. Now the enormous plot was covered in a splash of hovering lights over Yarmouth that had shifted uncertainly across the North Sea to the Scheldt. At that precise moment the line of lights was advancing to the north of Liège. A second line of lights had crossed the Zuider Zee at Juliandorf before abruptly changing course south-south-east at Lemmer on a projection that could bring it to Essen in the Ruhr.

General Kühnel, who wore a 1917 Iron Cross, and who was Duty Operations Officer on that particular night, stood nervously behind his desk, acutely aware that this was the worst part of any raid. The decision that he had to make now in deploying the Nightfighter forces would affect the whole future course of the air battle. Two questions had to be answered correctly to achieve this, and at the moment there was no answer to the second. Firstly, which of the streams moving smoothly across the plot was the Main Force and which were the spoofs, elaborately backed up with Window and other radar deception devices? Secondly, which city was the target?

Scattered throughout Germany were thirty radio and visual beacons, code-named after the phonetic alphabet: Anton, Berta, Cäsar, Dora, running from A to Z at random from the Elbe to the Danube. Once the bomber stream had entered Germany and its target was clear, the controllers could concentrate their nightfighting forces at the beacon nearest the target.

The background mush of sound within the Operations Theatre was somehow reminiscent of the distant sidetone on an overworked radio frequency, a constant flutter of searching concentration and anxious tension. Kühnel became aware that Folger, the Senior Liaison Officer, was standing beside him. Folger was a youngish man, inclined to fat, who had recently been seconded from Luftflotte South, after the North African evacuation, evacuation being, as everyone knew, a euphemism. Folger was the sort of man who was constantly pushing his point of view, hoping that someone more senior would take it up and act on it himself. In this way he would enhance his reputation if his opinion was proved right. On the other hand, he could disclaim responsibility if he was proved wrong.

'Where will it be, Folger? What's your opinion?'

Folger hesitated, apparently taken by surprise by the directness of the question at a time when it was, as both of them knew, much too early to give any kind of precise answer. Kühnel sometimes imagined that he had developed a nose for where the bomber stream might attack, but he only used it in an emergency and never in the face of apparent facts. Too many lives were at stake. He turned to Folger:

'Well, let's have it.'

'Not Berlin.'

'Not Berlin. If we're working backwards by elimination, we'll still be here tomorrow when the RAF's back for a return match.'

Folger produced what he considered to be an ace.

'You must have seen the afternoon's intelligence report, sir. There was a signal listed from Dublin. Scampton ordered short fuel loads for their Lancasters. That can only mean that they can't intend to go much beyond Kassel.'

Kühnel watched the implacable line of lights plunging like a slow-motion steel scalpel towards the vitals of Germany. He did not like intelligence reports. For one thing, people like Folger always produced them as some kind of infallible solution. Although it could be true that one tenuous, unconfirmed scrap of information could alter the course of a battle, probably never in the way the originating agent thought.

'Any change in the met?'

'No, sir. Four-tenths over Central Germany with a five-thousand-metre ceiling from Hannover down to Strassburg; the wind's still shifting north.'

A klaxon sounded over the loudspeaker.

'Alarm! Alarm! The bomber stream is dividing course 205 at Olno. Direction Clervaux.'

The message was simultaneously received in control rooms from Lübeck to the Swiss frontier.

'What do you think now?'

'Strassburg is usually a day target. No, that is a spoof.'

'What about the original situation?'

'Either Essen or Frankfurt or even Emsdorf. It's the same old trick, a feint in the north to draw off our fighters while the Main Force goes through.'

'Or the other way around.'

'I can't deny that.'

The centre spur of lights was almost at the Belgian frontier.

'However,' Folger went on, 'Himmelbett have sent out their mobiles and are now certain that the central bomber stream is the real thing, based on sound location. One can't argue with engine noises. That can't be a radar spoof.'

'They are dropping Window?'

'They are *all* dropping Window, north, south and centre. The central stream is on a bearing that will take them south of Liège between St Trond and Venlo. I think the target will be a Rhine town.'

The lights on the plot showed that the centre section of the bomber stream was on the point of crossing the frontier of the Third Reich.

Kühnel said:

'All Reich fighter units to converge on Beacon Ida. Announce stand-by on amber for the West Reich flak defences. Rheingold alert.'

Himmelbett Station Dormouse basically consisted of four Würzburg D short-range tracking radars, which were operated in conjunction with Nightfighter Control at 1 Gruppe Nachtjagdgeschwader[1] 3, Florennes, which that night included the Hainaut Squadron.

The Dormouse Station also had a Würzburg-Riese[2] installation nearby, the lattice-work 7.5-metre dish giving a range of fifty miles. Additionally Ansbach FuMG 68 gun-laying radar serviced 3/246 Battery of 154 Flak Regiment, together with its searchlight companies.

The whole complex was interspersed between the firing

[1] Nightfighter squadron.

[2] Giant Würzburg.

kilns and brick-fields of the Société Anonyme des Matériaux de Construction de Brabant, four and a half kilometres south-west of Charleroi.

Himmelbett Station Dormouse also consisted of an attached Luftwaffe signals squadron, including twenty-seven Luftwaffe auxiliaries to work the Würzburg sets. One of these was Christina Kellermann.

Although she did not particularly like the Belgians, whom she regarded as insincere, Christina endured the posting with good grace since she was only two and a half hours from Emsdorf if she took the *Lorelei* Express from Brussels.

She scanned the plot of the Würzburg D set she was operating and adjusted direction to the latest reported bearing of the bomber stream. Outside, the scanning dish traversed north eight degrees, revealing in the half-light the white-stencilled silhouettes of the three Stirlings and two Lancasters that had been confirmed kills.

Dormouse had been luckier than some, but not as lucky as others. The bomber streams tended to follow certain defined lanes as they approached Germany, prescribed by the flak-belts defending cities. This meant that Chicken, Moth and Baboon, scattered among the Nightfighter fields in the flat North European countryside had the better chance of tracking a maverick bomber from the stream, before talking on a white-and-grey dappled Me-110, its nose heavy with Lichtenstein dipoles, until, four miles from the target, the Nightfighter's RAD operator could pick up the bomber's plot.

Against the snowstorm blurring of Window Christina tuned the cathode.

'Dormouse One has a contact.'

Christina was one of the operators who had taught herself to read through Window, interpreting the faint but persistent signal that marked a genuine target, and expertly ironing out the disordered jumble of electronic peaks and troughs the interference generated.

'Dormouse One, the courier[1] is range 38 kilometres,

[1] target aircraft.

height 4000 metres, bearing 347.'

The Nightfighter controller said through her headphones:

'I am giving you Hänsel 24 kilometres, height 3600 metres, bearing 196.'

The telex chattered as the details of the anticipated duel were momentarily transformed into electrical pulses over the landline to Brown Bear. The third Würzburg D dish turned uncertainly almost due south as the operator began to track the hunting Nightfighter's course from Gembloux across the box to Beauvechaine.

Christina said excitedly:

'The courier is south of the stream, on the fringe of Window jamming.'

The Luftwaffe captain who was watchkeeper smiled indulgently. These girls were always the same. As excited as if they were spending an afternoon at the races. God knows there would be chances enough now and on the return flight.

He said soothingly:

'Just keep the plot and let Hänsel have the courier's course corrections.'

Suddenly the metallic resonance of the Control loudspeaker broke into the building tension of the RAD room:

'Condition Amber. Rheingold . . . Rheingold.'

Christina's concentration flagged for a moment, but she recovered the plot:

'Distance 25 kilometres. Height – no change of state. Bearing 385.'

Inge, the traffic clerk with the baby face and blonde curls, whispered:

'On that bearing it can only mean that Frankfurt's getting it again.'

Christina's heart missed a beat in spite of herself.

'Oh, I *am* sorry,' the girl added. 'I forgot.'

Emsdorf was the next large city after Frankfurt.

Somehow Christina could never associate her town with the heaps of rubble and the dead dust-storms of soot, ash and pulverized plaster that now formed a transient shroud over so many German cities – a shroud that could never seal in entirely the distasteful smell of death.

Emsdorf, as the Express passed through the ruins of Köln, Bonn and Koblenz, could never be as badly hit as that. It was an impossibility, for she had known every street, living there since she was a child. The war, although it had done many things, could not do that to her. Of course there had been raids, but the bombers had usually missed the target, diverted to the make-believe fires, flak and searchlights of the miniature decoy city, mocked up out of timber and corrugated iron, with a carefully excavated canal to simulate the river. Strung out like a permanent carnival fun-fair, unpopulated and out of season five miles from the suburbs. But through cloud at twenty thousand feet it had been Emsdorf often enough to the British air bombers.

She glanced from the Würzburg D monitor to the frosted glass of the plotting table, where the blue light of the Nightfighter was moving with a ponderous inexorability to intercept the slower-moving red light of the bomber.

'Hänsel predicts Lichtenstein contact in two minutes.'

The English bomber flew on, apparently oblivious to its almost inevitable fate, the drift easing it gently south across the plot.

The loudspeaker blared again:

'Condition Red Hesse. All Reichfighters assemble at Beacon Ida. Luftkommando Twelve Flak Units stand by. Early warning alarm Koblenz, Frankfurt, Mannheim . . .'

The wireless signal from Brown Bear broadcast on all channels suddenly dissolved into a high-pitched wail, as the frequency was overwhelmed by an insistent screaming modulation that drowned the broadcast signal.

The watchkeeper said:

'Why aren't we switched to landline?'

'We're out of spare pairs, sir. They've all been claimed by Nightfighters.'

While the operator moved furiously into the next emergency channel, Christina turned away to scan the plot once more and discovered with a mounting panic that the faint blue blip marking the courier had disappeared off the cathode.

She made a rapid search covering the last bearing to left and right by fifteen degrees. Finally she announced wearily, at the same time fighting back her tears:

'Dormouse One, there is no contact. It's the damned glare. They're so damned hard to keep tuned.'

The watchkeeper frowned slightly, but kept his patience, saying as he usually did on such occasions:

'The set must need servicing. What was the interference? Have you anything unusual?'

They had to be on constant alert against any new counter-radar devices.

'The set is performing normally,' Christina said in a flat voice and then bit her lip. The watchkeeper looked at her. It was obvious that she had had enough.

'You need a break. Go and get yourself a cup of coffee from the canteen. Auxiliary Losse can take over your desk.'

Then he added for the benefit of the Nightfighter controller:

'Sorry about that, Hänsel. We'll find you another courier in a minute.'

But what's the good of that? Christina thought, as she stumbled through the darkness towards the blue-shaded light of the canteen. It was a big raid. There could be six hundred or even more ploughing remorselessly on across the Rhine and past the Frankfurt defence-zone to Emsdorf.

She decided she must not think about it any more. Some other town was sure to get it. She was all nerves. But the chicory coffee tasted sour and sugarless, and her fingers clattered the cup against the saucer as she tried to put out of her mind what could happen before the night was over.

9

Tame Sow

Maitland entered in the navigator's log:

'11.09 hrs. Sergeant McIndoe, air-gunner, died from flak wounds.'

Then he rubbed out 'died' and inserted 'found dead' in its place. He sat for several minutes staring incredulously at his own meticulous pencil entry, stunned by its sense of total finality at the end of the other formal and predictable entries. It was as though an idiot had suddenly interposed his grotesque and bloody thumbprint at the bottom of a half-completed illuminated manuscript.

Maitland had no desire to discover what 'found dead' involved, although it would have been different if McIndoe had only been wounded. From now on, McIndoe no longer counted as a person, and next trip they would fly with a new air-gunner. He closed the navigator's log as he heard Hunting's voice over the intercom:

'Pilot to Navigator, position check, please.'

Maitland now discovered that his mind was racing, so that it was difficult to concentrate with the subconscious knowledge that McIndoe was lying dead somewhere aft of the wing root. He welcomed the illusion of security and detachment his blacked-out compartment gave him.

The pitter-patter of wire brushes rustling along the duralumin fuselage skin, flickering below the port side of the unarmoured upper turret in a cascade of exploding needles, had lacerated the right-hand side of McIndoe's flying helmet and electrically heated flying suit in a hiss of shrapnel that severed his tibial and femoral arteries so that very soon he lost consciousness and bled to death. His blood spurting and draining away down his right leg, as he sat crouched in his seat, to form a pool behind the main spar steps.

Maitland pulled himself together.

'Maastricht coming up to port. We should cross into the Fatherland in fifteen minutes.'

If he stretched out beyond the curtain, he could see the pink luminescence of the Ruhr valley to the north-east, its industrial haze lit up by curtain after curtain of searchlight beams.

Then he heard Fairclough say:

'Cap, can the Nav give me a hand with McIndoe? I'm trying to pull the poor sod out of his turret.'

'Go and help him sort it out, Professor.'

Maitland said nothing, although he thought it a breach of professional etiquette for the navigator, crouched in his ivory castle, to be involved in anything other than a total emergency. It was questionable whether a dead gunner, jammed in his turret, constituted a total emergency.

Maitland was shocked by the scene in the fuselage behind Fairclough's station. McIndoe had been sitting on his parachute while he had been alive, and this had now jammed against his thighs as the wireless operator tried to extricate his trunk through the horizontal turret port.

The rubber soles of Maitland's loose-fitting suede flying boots slithered in the blood as he shouted:

'For Christ's sake, what are you trying to do?'

Fairclough's battledress top was covered in McIndoe's blood.

'Get the poor sod out, of course.'

'Why not leave him there?'

The flak had fretted a fine tracery along the fuselage, through which Maitland occasionally glimpsed the brilliant flicker of the inner port exhausts. He held himself steady by gripping one of the flare racks. From the solemn predictability of the periodic routine checks and fixes and the certain confirmation of his own plot, the operation had assumed a chaotic, nightmare overtone.

First the iced-up engine and now death. Not formal and respectable death with candles, lilies and an undertaker, but squalid, unforeseen and undignified death with a gallon of McIndoe's blood washing about on the rear fuselage floor. As Fairclough heaved at the trunk, the side of the flying suit split, revealing long gashes of bloody muscle and white bone and an ugly flapping tear in the stomach wall.

'Don't be a bloody clot. We're not even halfway there yet. Someone may have to use these guns.'

'What do you want me to do?'

Shrapnel had peppered the parallels of ducts inside the fuselage, so that it was impossible to say what damage the trunking might conceal. Behind the punctured metal-work could be a half-severed cable or fouled control wheel to jam the rudder or elevators.

'Get him out, for Christ's sake!'

When he concentrated, Maitland could immediately see the cause of the problem, the obvious fact that McIndoe's bulky parachute was preventing them from retrieving his body.

He reached up distastefully past an area of torn flesh to the parachute harness turn-buckle, moving it clockwise to release the main webbing, so that McIndoe's body now dropped another eighteen inches before the parachute pack jammed once more at the nape of his lolling neck. However, it no longer proved difficult for the two men to guide McIndoe's head and shoulders back down the turret port entry.

When McIndoe was free, his hollow-eyed corpse's face turned woodenly towards the fuselage formers. Maitland pulled the rip-cord of the parachute and began to tug at the canopy.

'What the hell's that in aid of?'

'The blood.'

Maitland carefully arranged the white silk canopy along the sticky metal criss-cross hatching of the floor and heaped the shrouds beside McIndoe's body. The white silk turned to brown in patches. Then Maitland said to Fairclough:

'Shouldn't we lay him on the stretcher?'

'To hell with that. He's too messy, and it makes no difference to him where he is now, poor sod. Save the luxuries for someone who has a high survival factor.'

In the end they propped up McIndoe by the rear-turret ammunition chute, using the parachute pack to hide the grim indecency of his wounds. There were bloodstains down the fuselage walls below the upper turret that could be seen even in the half-light. Maitland would have preferred to wipe them clean, but there was nothing to do it with, and besides there was no time. Glancing at his watch he saw it was 11.14. In two minutes he should get a fix on the junction of the River Sauer with the Moselle, so that he could check the drift.

Fairclough sat down at his station, grateful for once for the hot blast of the heater, which, maintaining a constant temperature in excess of 100 degrees, made it the warmest part of the aircraft.

Back at the console he began to make a routine check on the R 1155 receiver, working his way through the list of German Nightfighter frequencies. As he searched with the turning dial he suddenly heard a German operator:

'This is Hänsel. Where the hell are you, Gretel?'

'South of Liège. The DB was playing up on pre-flight. That's why I didn't RV as planned.'

Another voice broke in:

'Keep looking. You're in the middle of the stream.'

The voices began to fade off the frequency, as Fairclough's hand hovered over the master oscillator of the 'tinsel' jammer before thinking better of it.

'I'm picking up Luftwaffe Nightfighter chatter, Cap. What's more, it's strength 10.'

There was a pause as Hunting digested the unwelcome news. There was nothing surprising in the fact that they were picking up German R/T. What was less welcome was the knowledge that they were receiving the signal at maximum strength. This could only mean that the Nightfighter was much too close for comfort. An operator of Fairclough's experience was unlikely to be wrong about that.

He glanced at the Boozer[1] lights on the control panel in front of him. An orange light would mean they were being

[1] RAF passive receiver tuned to Lichtenstein/Würzburg frequencies.

tracked by a radar ground station. The red light would mean that they were being hunted by a radar-equipped Nightfighter. Both lights were neutral.

'I'm taking to the clouds. Keep your eyes open, everyone.' But as he eased back the stick he felt buffeting at the tail plane as the altimeter suddenly registered a fifty- and then a hundred-foot drop as the thirty-two tons of Lancaster hit a sudden patch of turbulence.

Maitland said:

'Air pocket. We're crossing the Ardennes.'

The same patch of turbulence, induced by down-draughts of cold air against the hills and hollows of the Ardennes, was also experienced by Major Krasnatsky in Hänsel, as his wireless operator anxiously kept a radio watch on Gretel's frequency. Apart from missing Lange, which had ruffled Krasnatsky, there had only been one firm contact during this patrol, which had been loused up by the ineptitude of the Dormouse Würzburg operator. It seemed unlikely that there was any immediate prospect of another kill.

Hogel was also engaged in irritably freelancing the surrounding airspace in the hope of picking up the lost contact.

'I'm turning now,' said Krasnatsky with a giggle. 'I don't want to take any chances over these hills. And where the hell's Gretel got to?'

As he spoke, Krasnatsky's canopy was momentarily blotted out by a giant dark shadow, flickering with stabs of flame. The Major instinctively threw up his right arm to protect himself, as he heard the sudden roar and the Nightfighter bucked wildly in the wake of the turbulence left by the prop wash of the four-engined heavy bomber.

Krasnatsky pushed the control column forward between his knees, as the silhouette hovered momentarily as though to drop and crush them and then disappeared, leaving tiny flickers of flame impressed for a few seconds on the Major's single retina.

The Nightfighter pilot immediately banked and started to climb into the now empty sky as Hogel shouted excitedly:

'We're in business! That fat dog. Did you see that fat dog?'

Krasnatsky answered coldly, since he always felt uneasy when confronted with such emotional displays from his subordinates:

'Of course I saw it, Hogel. Now you can catch it for me in one of your wonder boxes.'

'I'd like to try the Flensburg as well as the Lichtenstein.'

'You can do what the hell you like so long as you bring me a visual contact.'

As Barton opened his eyes momentarily to escape from his sense of vertigo, attempting to focus on something that was substantial and constant and which did not move, he was not certain whether the grey shadow that fell behind them was real, or only another illusion, invented by his brain in isolation, like the cloud wisps that were forever changing to recognition silhouettes and back to nothing after a second or two, before he had time to focus on them properly.

When the Lancaster began to climb, Barton's stomach heaved as the tail plane rose and fell and a sudden vicious plunge left his stomach suspended in mid-air. He cleared his throat which was dry with nausea and tried to eliminate the salt taste that kept returning to his mouth.

Then he said, exercising great control, so that none of the others would guess that anything was wrong:

'I say, Cap. I think you almost pranged a Nightfighter.'

'Theirs or ours?'

'I'm not kidding. Somewhere out in the bluey behind.'

Hunting said:

'Eddie, you better man the rear upper, in case it won't go away.'

'Wilco, Cap.'

Looking back tensely across the night sky, where he rode alone and in darkness like a sinner on his way to hell,

Barton felt that he was being transported through some black diabolic roller-coaster tunnel backwards, and dying inch by inch over a mad chaos of flashing lights and distant searchlight fingers. His stomach heaved again.

'Eddie, do you have a reading on Monica[1]?'

'There's nothing I can see, but I'll have to fiddle about with the set to be sure.'

'Nothing this end either,' said Hunting. 'Are you sure you didn't dream the whole thing up?'

Nursing his misery, Barton did not choose to reply.

Maitland made a log entry, at the same time preventing his teeth from chattering by clenching them together by an effort of will.

'23.44 hrs. EA Nightfighter sighted on collision course. South of St Trond. 5.20 east. 50.30 north.'

He spent some time thinking about this entry since it took his mind off what could happen in the next five minutes.

He finally decided to leave the entry as it was, recognizing that it might be important to report their proximity to the nearest Luftwaffe Nightfighter station. It was also valid to give the bearing of the near-collision, since, if they were shot down and his log was found with the entry, it would help the searchers locate the aircraft and recover their bodies.

Then he heard Collins say:

'I better move into the forward turret. O.K., Cap?'

Hunting had begun to corkscrew, diving and climbing to port and starboard, and, because of the buffeting, Maitland was aware that they were approaching the front, which as predicted should give them heavier cloud cover over Germany. Not that there was much comfort to him in the thought, since because of Hunting's unpredictable evasive tactics it was more than likely that they would deviate from course and it would now be out of the question to hope for an accurate fix at the junction of the Sauer and the Moselle.

[1] Radar for rear warning.

His charts and instruments skittered backwards and forwards over his table, reflecting the erratic movements of the aircraft, and Maitland cursed the fresh disorder with a rising sense of inner panic.

The red Boozer light winked malevolently on at the top of Hunting's panel. The sergeant pilot made no comment, although Howells' pupils dilated in fear and he turned his head desperately to left and right, as though looking for some way of escape through the Perspex window panels.

'We have them now,' said Hogel with a tone of finality, for he was rarely known to lose a contact. 'The Flensburg is clearer than the Lichtenstein, but I am getting an unusual modulation on it, an oscillation on the upper lateral. The operator cannot have tuned in his set.'

'Skip the technical details,' Krasnatsky said. 'Take me in on the SN-2.'

Hogel made a rapid mental calculation. The Me-110 would be flying at almost three times the speed of the English heavy bomber on its pursuit course. At 360 mph the Nightfighter should in any case make a visual contact in the next sixty seconds. This could mean a danger of overshooting.

'You better reduce to 200.' The two plots on the SN-2 cathode were by this time almost perfectly in conjunction and the blue cross centred also on the Flensburg cathode.

'For you, Hogel, nothing is too much trouble.'

Krasnatsky giggled nervously as he pulled back the throttles.

Forty seconds later, Krasnatsky saw the dark shadow of the Lancaster as it wove across the sky ahead of them, although it was easier to pick out the heat off the four grey engine nacelle pods through the infra-red sight.

'It is not cricket, but I shall take him from behind. First we must eliminate the tail-gunner.'

The Lancaster reached the zenith of its latest corkscrew cycle, fourteen thousand, one hundred and seventy-three feet over the Teufelskopf, one of the line of peaks in the Schwarzwälder Hochwald, that ran parallel to the high Hunsrück plateau.

At almost this point exactly, the front drifting out lazily from behind the Rhine met the icy high-altitude winds that had passed through Stavanger early that morning. These winds met the rising air-currents off the warm forests of the Saarland and the Pfalz at the German frontier.

For this reason the buffeting at the back of P for Peter increased and, when added to Hunting's slow corkscrew motion, became unbearable so far as Barton was concerned.

As the Lancaster paused before descending into the trough, Barton ripped off his oxygen mask and vomited abruptly into the well of the Frazer Nash Turret, hanging with both hands from the .303 Brownings and their hydraulic mechanisms, sobbing with terror and humiliation, his forehead pressed against the icy turret Perspex.

The air, at least, felt cold and clear in his throat as he gasped for breath. But when he opened his eyes, he saw once more the low oncoming profile of a Nightfighter increasing in size from moment to moment. There was no time for him to retrieve his oxygen mask, as he depressed the Brownings and guided the sight to the nose of the attacking plane as it dipped in a shallow dive before climbing to the roller-coaster attack.

The flash of Barton's tracer did not affect Fairclough's night sight, although he was surprised by the fact that under his silk gloves he had no feeling in his fingers. It was all the more surprising because he had only been inside the upper turret for five minutes and still felt warm from the cabin heat in the bottom half of his body. However, when he reached for the turret traverse clutch, nothing happened and it was the same when he pressed the gun button.

'He has a lot to learn,' said Krasnatsky with a giggle as the rear-gunner's tracer floated harmlessly past the attacking Me-110. 'To open fire at four hundred metres is throwing away ammunition. Well, he shall have his first and only lesson.'

'New, new,' shouted Hogel. 'Greenhorns straight out of Bomberkommando Gunnery School.'

He watched the flickering oscillation on the Flensburg. This target must have a special characteristic.

'Let's make them all wish they hadn't forgotten their invitation cards,' Krasnatsky said. 'Victory. Compliments of the Third Reich.'

For a moment it seemed to Krasnatsky that the target reared up to make a giant cross, but then, as he pressed the firing button of his four nose cannon, the bomber vanished abruptly from his sights. One minute the four grey white engine pods were firmly fixed in the infra-red, the next moment there was nothing.

Krasnatsky's worst fears were confirmed as he saw the retrograde descent of the altimeter needle.

'Scheiss Heil! The descent into Hell. A hundred metres in ten seconds must almost be an Olympic record.'

The sudden bumps continued as Krasnatsky kept on the course originally set by Hogel.

'Will we get another turn in the shooting gallery?'

'There's a fault in the Lichtenstein, probably all this buffeting, but the Flensburg's still giving out a signal.'

The signal was fading, but Hogel could still make out the characteristic oscillation that singled out this target.

Suddenly Krasnatsky heard Lange over his headphones.

'We're to proceed to Beacon Ida. It's a general order. I'll meet up with you there at twelve and a half thousand.'

The crew of P for Peter were still recovering from the sudden and unexpected descent caused by the down-draught as the north wind plunged through and below the warm front now restlessly contorting over Rheinhessen.

'What happened to you, Barton? Why didn't you give us all a shout?'

'I was adjusting my mask.'

There was an awkward silence. They had all flown with him long enough to be able to guess what that implied.

'Did you miss taking your Farnborough tablet or something?'

Barton did not want to discuss what had happened now that it was all over or seemed to be.

'I reckon I got one in on the bastard.'

'Reckon? Reckon?' Hunting replied. 'Be bloody sure you did next time.'

The Lancaster rattled and moaned, passing through the turbulence above the Rhine valley.

It was a long time before any of them spoke. Now they were quite happy to sit in the quiet, unbroken darkness to the south of Koblenz, listening to the solid roar of the engines.

All, that is, except Fairclough, who almost screamed with pain as he rubbed the tips of his frostbitten fingers in the warmth of the cabin heater.

10

Bomb Run

'Cranwell' Collins felt cold in spite of the steady current of hot air pumped through the forward half of the Lancaster's fuselage by the cabin heater. Even although underneath his sidcot suit and chamois overgloves he was wearing a second pair of silk gloves and had also followed the recommended practice of wearing next to his skin a pair of silk stockings borrowed from a girl friend. Girl friend was, perhaps, too concrete a description, since Collins had returned from a bottle party at the 'Bag o' Nails' in Soho after a week-end leave with the stockings both as a trophy and an excuse.

However, the cold, stiff feeling he had lying along the brown leatherette air bomber's couch began to be forgotten and his heart began to race as Hunting banked precisely, and without skid, at the yellow marker blazing in a potato field to the south of Friedberg.

It was already time for him to complete his last-minute checks, for on the bombing run P for Peter would be travelling at one hundred and eighty miles an hour at ten thousand feet. There was no time now for them to attempt to gain the correct bombing height. The distance from Friedberg to where the red and green target indicators glowed on the Emsdorf recreation ground was just under ten miles, and therefore, since they were travelling at three miles a minute, they would reach the target in three minutes and twenty seconds.

The sky over Emsdorf and the undulating hills of Rheinhessen were not, however, totally free from cloud, although the cloud base of strato-cumulus was still sufficiently broken to allow Collins to pick out woods, valleys and the rolling unfenced fields of the countryside.

Meanwhile as Hunting pussied in and out of the cloud base, the air bomber became aware of a luminescence penetrating the cloud which became the dazzling glare of a hundred and fifty-three searchlight beams as the Lancaster dropped below its cover.

At the same time, Collins became more and more aware of the flak, which triggered off the irrational feeling that it was being aimed at him personally behind the ground optical glass of the nose sighting-panel. This was understandable enough, crouched as he was over the Mark XIV bombsight with its collimator poised to project its cruciform image onto the graticule glass in front of the dumpy twelve-inch cylinder which adjusted the constantly varying information fed into it from the flexible drives of the computer.

The flak reminded Collins of the firework display at his prep school on Coronation night, six years before, except that it was indiscriminate and silent against the constantly throbbing roar of the four Merlin engines.

Lying at his station with his teddy-bear propped up beside him, Collins was overcome by a strange mixture of fear, exhilaration and power, which made him determined to conquer the moral deterrent offered by the flak and put his bombs down, right on target.

If he moved to the left, he could feel the computer unit in its cage against his thigh. He had already set this for wind-speed and direction and made the necessary adjustment to take the terminal velocities of the bomb load into account.

The bomb load consisted of the single four-thousand-pound high capacity cookie filled with minol, that lay slung at the centre and occupying over twenty-five per cent of the thirty-three-feet-long bomb-bay; fourteen SBCs, each container holding one hundred and three 4-lb incendiaries, their narrow two-feet long magnesium alloy cases filled with thermite, so that they did not look like bombs at all, but innocent octagonal metal bars. Lastly there were six 500-pound 'J' petrol bombs.

The other factors that the computer processed were fed into it directly from the relevant instruments: the altimeter reading, the D/R compass course and the indicated air-speed.

On the approach, the computer would constantly adjust the predicted trajectory of the bombs to any new flight situation, and all that Collins would have to do would be to follow the light image projected on the graticule glass in the form of a reversed cross. The long vertical line indicated drift and should coincide with the track of the aircraft; the short horizontal line towards its base was the release line. When the centre of this cross reached the aiming point shown by the burning target indicators, he could operate the bomb release, confident that the bomb load would fall with a large degree of certainty within the target area.

After they had turned at Friedberg, Collins switched the main control of the automatic controls to 'out' and also turned on the bombsight cock. Next he activated the computer and graticule, after resetting wind, speed and direction on the computer.

'O.K., Cap. This is it.'

'Right, Collins. Bomb doors open. It's all yours.'

Collins felt excitement surge within him. For the next

one hundred and fifty seconds, Hunting would be steering the Lancaster onto the track that Collins dictated, using his detailed target map to begin with, and later using the sight as the target area moved within the area of the graticule image to bring the target down the drift line.

There was nothing else. Collins had positively fused as they crossed the Channel.

Apart from an error in map reading, the only risk of inaccurate bombing would occur if the Lancaster was forced to bank in excess of sixty degrees or dive at an angle in excess of forty. The result of these changes in the aircraft's state would be to topple the computer's gyros and invalidate the sum of the factors that had been fed into it, until they were reset.

However, provided there was no drastic change of attitude, any evasive action within these limits would not impair the accuracy of the bombing. So long as a steady, though not necessarily straight flight was maintained for a few seconds before release, the bomb load would fall within the intended area.

Collins said:

'What's the altitude, Cap?'

'Nine and a quarter.'

At just under two miles high they were now below the cloud base, although from time to time they still passed through a ball of cumulus. Ahead, Collins could see the target indicators, invisibly reinforced at two minute intervals by the backers-up from the Pathfinder squadron. The cascades of crimson and green pyrotechnics stood out in front of the harsh orange glow and the dense smoke clouds that were already rising over Emsdorf.

Collins said excitedly:

'There are two big fires and I can see the bridges. The target's well away.'

Collins was still aware of the artificial full-moon luminescence in the sky surrounding them, so that it was possible to follow their track across the dark wooded undulations of the Unterwald and the long white ribbons of the Autobahnen. The searchlight batteries had every intention of making the individual Main Force bombers stand out against the cloud, as exposed as flies wandering across a newly whitewashed ceiling.

Collins steered Hunting down the Autobahn. When it was absorbed in the long avenues leading to the centre of the old city, they would almost be up to the target indicators, and at that point Collins decided that they would turn onto the precise bombing bearing.

Glancing through the port panel, Collins caught sight of a black silhouette in profile half a mile away and perhaps five hundred feet lower. It seemed to him clearly lit in the unnatural glare of the searchlights, so much so that he could almost make out the squadron markings. Even as he watched, a lane of flak boxed in the Lancaster to the front and sides and in agony he waited to see if the pilot would change height and course within the nineteen seconds' grace allowed by the German flak predictors and gunners. The heavy bomber, however, continued to maintain its track, regardless of the walls of flak building up around it.

Suddenly there was a silent scarlet explosion that seemed to sprout from the bomb-bay below the wing spars and seconds later he heard what seemed the rattle of wreckage against P for Peter's port wing.

Then he heard Hunting over the intercom.

'What's the matter, Collins? Finger trouble? I'm currently driving this bus to your order.'

'We're on track, Cap. Just keep her steady.'

A moment later he added:

'Did you see that, Cap? An aircraft bought it just now. They must have hit the cookie.'

'I can't help that,' Hunting said. 'I'm too busy trying to do my job.'

'Left a bit, Cap, left, steady. Turn on one twenty magnetic.'

Collins pushed aside his target map. At the edge of the graticule glass he could see the TIs as unearthly fountains of constantly cascading fire before the flaring darkness beyond.

Collins tried to erase the memory of what he had just seen from his mind, although his retina carried the reverse green negative of the exploding Lancaster for several seconds. As they crept closer to the target, his night vision returned and he picked out a constant ripple of explosions across the town as other invisible heavies deposited their two-ton cookies. The topography of Emsdorf now stood out like a street map in fiery orange and yellow, the bright, near-white veins of the streets a blazing network as they ran to the river's edge through the clearly demarcated circle of the ancient city walls.

The air bomber had little time to be appalled by what he saw, since with a great mental and nervous effort he was engaged in fighting his rising fear and hatred of the funfair-brilliant flak that rose to meet the Main Force. This added a grotesque light-hearted carnival feeling to the miles of blazing buildings below. Fighting wave after wave of fear, he felt his scrotum retract.

'Keep her steady, Cap. Starboard a point. Hold it.'

Collins groped for the Mickey Mouse behind the bomb release guard in the half-lit shadows of his station and removed the cable and button release from the air bomber's panel.

Now the inverted graticule cross was approaching the crimson and green cluster of the steadily burning target indicators.

'Hold her steady, Cap. Hold it.'

When he pressed the bomb release button at the end of the Mickey Mouse, the Lancaster only shook slightly without the dramatic upsurge he had learned to expect with the release of the full seven-ton bomb load.

However, he threw the camera switch, waiting for the first red light to come up on his panel.

'Hold her on track. Stand by for photoflash.'

As the red light blipped on, he released the 150lb photoflash bomb whose barometric fuse would automatically detonate the magnesium charge to give 2,400 million candlepower at seven thousand feet, capturing the explosion of P for Peter's cookie and the pattern of impacting incendiaries and 'J' bombs for the automatic camera.

Below him, tiny pinpoints of light marked the shower of fourteen hundred four-pound incendiaries that had dropped away from their containers, within a quarter-mile radius of St Matthias, Goethestrasse and Baum Weg.

Collins heard Hunting say:

'I didn't see our cookie.'

'Neither did I. I'll check the board. Maybe it's hung up on us.'

'Sod that game of soldiers,' Barton interrupted over the intercom. 'Don't tell me that on our first demonstration of sex-appeal bombing we're still fucking about over the target with a gash two-ton load of minol?'

'Just keep your eyes peeled for Nightfighters,' Hunting said.

'The panel light's still on,' Collins said tensely.

'Right. I'm orbiting back on the fire marker,' Hunting said. 'In the meantime I suggest you find out just what went wrong.'

Over the intercom all of them heard a curious embarrassing sound that electrified everyone in the aircraft. Howells, the flight engineer, wiping the sweat off his forehead with his chamois gloved hand, had inadvertently switched on his mike toggle, set in the rubber face-piece of his oxygen mask. For several seconds the crew of P for Peter were compelled to listen to the flight engineer's moaning sobs, as he sat rocking by his panel, his head buried in his arms in terror.

'Cut that out,' Hunting said sharply. 'None of us feel very bright right now.'

The sound of Howells' irrational sobs, which had begun to unman them all, abruptly ceased.

By now P for Peter had crossed the river and Hunting banked slowly north-west over the eastern suburbs of the city on a course that would take them back to the Friedberg marker.

As he did so, Collins, to his horror, discovered the cause of the hang-up. Out of all the actions he thought he had so thoroughly and meticulously performed, and of all the checks that he had carried out, he had by an oversight omitted to throw the slip heater switch which would have prevented the freezing of the 400-lb-bomb release mechanism.

He immediately threw the switch. And then as some kind of alibi to himself, or an excuse of physical activity to cover his own fear and confusion, he wriggled to the back of his station to the bomb-bay inspection port, where, silhouetted against the dull orange flicker of the burning city, the nine-foot boiler-like canister of the two-ton high capacity bomb still hung menacingly.

For a moment he felt the urge to disguise the cause of their present predicament by saying that the heater circuit had gone u/s, and then he decided against it. He felt his mouth go dry, as he spoke down the intercom.

'I'm sorry, Cap. I've put up a king-size black. The bloody bomb-slip heater isn't switched.'

Hunting's reply was studiously neutral:

'O.K., Collins. Get it fixed for second time round.'

By now the plane was turning over the railway sidings and the industrial complex that lay to the north of Emsdorf, which so far had not yet suffered any great damage from the first wave attack.

Collins, desperate to make things right, said:

'I'll double-check the circuit fuse.'

A gloomy silence fell on the crew. The prospect of a second bomb run did nothing to encourage them.

Then, over the intercom, Collins heard Howells say:

'I'll go forward and check, Cap. O.K.?'

There was a silence before Hunting said:

'O.K., Howells. You go forward.'

The Lancaster flew on round the periphery of the city, escaping the detailed attention of the main defences which were concentrating their efforts on the bomb run of the bomber stream as the individual aircraft criss-crossed the target indicators at different angles of attack, although, from time to time, they were all aware of bursts of erratic light and medium flak.

Collins said:

'We'll make it second time round, Cap. There'll be no problem.'

Barton said:

'The officer writes epitaphs too.'

Collins was now aware of the figure of the flight engineer crouching down through the narrow access port which led to the air bomber's compartment. He had removed his oxygen mask, but was clutching a parachute. He sat for a moment at the bottom of the stairs. Then, over the roar of the engine, Collins heard him shout:

'You've no hope of fixing that bloody bomb-release in time.'

'What the hell d'you mean?'

'Hunting says we've to abandon the aircraft. Bale out.'

Collins became aware of a suppressed hysteria behind Howells' words. Then, as though to convince him finally, Howells added:

'The inner port's lit up like a Roman candle. Unless we jump now, we'll never make it.'

'Make it where?'

'If I have to choose between the Stalag and being burned alive, I know which gets my vote.'

Ignoring Collins, the flight engineer made his way to the back of the compartment and began to turn the handles on the forward escape hatch.

'What's going on, Cap? Howells said there's an order to abandon.'

'He's talking a load of crap. Tell him to extract fingers and get back to his station.'

However, by now Howells had released the escape hatch catches and was buckling on his parachute as a gale of icy air howled in through the air bomber's compartment.

Collins shouted:

'Now just hang on a minute, Howells.'

'I'm not staying here to be fried alive, courtesy of Pilot Officer Prune and that bloody madman, Hunting.'

Collins grabbed at Howells' arm in the narrow confines of the compartment, but the flight engineer threw him off with so much force that Collins lost his balance and crashed across the couch, clutching at the Mark XIV bomb-sight as he felt the downstream suction from the escape hatch.

'Fuck off and win yourself a posthumous V.C., Collins. I'm not staying to see it happen.'

'Don't be a bloody fool. We're going to need you to make it back.'

'Not sodding likely. I'm not having any sodding gussie writing my ticket to sodding certain death.'

When Collins looked back over his shoulder, he could see that Howells was sitting at the edge of the escape hatch and that his legs, caught in the suction of the slipstream, were already sliding through the opening. Then, as he lost his balance, he clawed at Collins, gripping his right-hand flying boot, and the Pilot Officer instinctively caught hold of the bomb aimer's panel, his hand falling on the bomb-release and inadvertently pressing the button.

For this reason, as Howells left the aircraft, his exit coincided with the release of the four-thousand-pound bomb. As the Lancaster suddenly surged up, both of them fell away into the darkness.

However, Sergeant Howells was now unconscious, since the small of his back had struck the port bomb door of P for Peter. He also made a slower descent since his terminal velocity was only 1200 feet per second. Moments before, the two-ton cookie had already reached its terminal velocity of 3,800 feet a second.

As a result, Howells regained momentary consciousness five seconds later after leaving the plane, three thousand feet above Emsdorf, before relapsing into unconsciousness once more, after having been aware that he was apparently hovering over a sea of fire as he vainly attempted to locate his parachute release handle.

The four-thousand-pound cookie fell in a different trajectory, carried back three hundred yards to the south-west by the wind, ripping open the roof of the neoprene storage bay of Gummi A.G. The resulting explosion fractured sixteen feeder lines of liquid acetylene which immediately combined with the surrounding oxygen to form a large unstable pocket of explosive gas. At the same time the four-thousand-pound bomb shorted out three main power cables servicing the vat heaters and power circuits, and the resulting arc to earth acted as a perfect detonator to the volatile chemical gas cloud, so that an uncontrollable fire was soon raging through the manufacturing, transport and storage bays. As the burning sheets of neoprene rubber began to melt, they crept along the floors of the complex like the overflow of a volcanic eruption, causing further fires and explosions, the flames driven constantly onwards by the prevailing wind.

Collins said:

'We're no longer hung up, Cap, but we've lost our flight engineer.'

Hunting had noted an imbalance in the stability of the Lancaster when the opening of the escape hatch had created new aerodynamic stresses that caused P for Peter's nose to lift.

'Too bad about Howells. You better man the forward turret, Collins. It'll be draughty where you are right now.'

Collins did not argue, both ashamed and thankful at what had taken place. So far as the others were concerned, the matter was probably closed, for the moment at any rate, and now was not the time for post mortems. However, he was acutely dissatisfied with his performance, which had put all of them at risk, so much so that he was unable to blame Howells for his precipitate exit.

11

Flak

Since he was now east of the target area, it seemed logical to Hunting to orbit the Friedberg marker before joining the inward bomber stream track that would return across the Low Countries, south of Brussels and north of Lille and over the Channel to the North Foreland and Reading.

Hunting knew that there were many captains who would deliberately avoid the disconnected stream on the flight home, preferring the illusory safety of isolation, but the sergeant pilot could see the sense in keeping up with the Main Force, which should inevitably reduce the odds against enemy attack. In any case, to turn west across the target now, as it flamed and smoked to port, would be to run the additional risk of collision or overbombing from the second wave Lancasters now crossing Emsdorf at twenty thousand feet and bombing through the broken layer of strato-cumulus which was already dispersing through the upward convection currents generated by the fires below.

As P for Peter crossed the Autobahn, Hunting sensed the feeling of relief running through the bomber, as the crew began to relax, now that the worst was over and they had at least reached the target and completed what they had set out to do.

Maitland entered in the navigator's log:

'0.29 hrs. Two-ton cookie released. Many good fires observed. Little flak.'

Fifteen seconds later, the spring-wound mechanical time fuse of an 88-mm round reached the correct predetermined position and released the firing pin, which, in its turn, instantaneously activated the booster detonator, through the flash hole, into the TNT charge, disintegrating the eighteen pounds of steel casing seventy-five feet above the starboard wing of P for Peter. The flak shell exploded upwards in a fan-like arc, some lower segments of which, travelling at a velocity of three miles a second, dispersed one pound of red-hot steel fragments across the fuselage and starboard wing root, ricochetting off the armour plate behind Hunting's seat and slashing the electrical trunking that ran beside the flight engineer's panel, shorting out four power circuits; so that soon fire was licking along the melting PVC towards the navigator's table. Other fragments interrupted the direction finder loop circuit and ploughed through the steel case of the main transmitter, shattering two valves.

In a matter of seconds, the fuselage forward became dark with thick, acrid chemical smoke, clouding the Perspex of the astrodome and the cockpit canopy.

The force of the explosion dropped the Lancaster's starboard wing and the aircraft yawed and side-slipped through four thousand feet. Maitland and Fairclough were flung off their seats by the sudden change of altitude as the starboard wing knifed down towards the centre of the burning city. Hunting struggled with the controls to regain the correct flying attitude as the fire, fanned by the draught through the forward escape hatch, roared across into the navigator's compartment, while the Lancaster began to buck and groan from the explosion of nearby flak-bursts and Hunting could feel the hot breath of fire at the back of his neck.

As he picked himself up, Maitland could scarcely believe the chaotic disorder that had suddenly invaded the black, curtained isolation of his compartment. Flames ran up the curtain, and the fire was greedily consuming the roll of maps that had lain neatly to the left of the table. Worse still, smoke was now pouring from the Gee nav box. Maitland seized the pyrene extinguisher and frantically pumped the handle, flooding the compartment with carbon dioxide as the flames flared blue-violet when the oxygen economizer lead exploded. Maitland then methodically proceeded to eliminate other minor fires in the code-book stowage, the parachute beside his plotting table, the window curtains and the trunking around the flight engineer's panel, at the same time respraying the charred and smouldering electrical conduits.

Maitland heard Barton say uneasily over the intercom:

'Can someone fill me in on what's happening?'

Hunting said:

'That's what we'd all like to know. How are things down your end?'

'Looks like bonfire night downstairs. If we go any lower, we'll see the fire engines.'

The sergeant pilot said:

'How are you doing, Maitland?'

'I don't know, but the fire's out this end.'

'It's O.K., chaps. We're still airborne,' Collins interjected.

Hunting said:

'You better come back and stand in as flight engineer.'

'What's the matter?' Barton asked anxiously. 'Has Howells been hit?'

'Actually no, old boy. Didn't you hear? He decided to pay an unplanned visit to the Third Reich.'

After a pause Barton said incredulously:

'Well, stone the crows! What else don't I know about?'

It was at that moment that Hunting, his heart in his throat, realized that half the instrument panel seemed to be dead. The air-speed indicator registered a constant 183 mph without a flicker of the needle. The altimeter was frozen at 9,350 feet, and the artificial horizon remained a rigid and unbending line.

Hunting felt beads of sweat forming on his forehead. Then, as the ASI and altimeter remained motionless, he increased throttle and began to climb.

In the light of this new development, the alternative courses that now lay open all appeared equally unattractive. Now he felt that he could no longer risk turning north-west across the turbulent hills of the Ardennes with the returning bombers of Main Force, while, on the other hand, to fly across France, south of the Stenay gap, over comparatively open ground, would involve a solo crossing of the primary German Nightfighter belt to the north of Paris, which was equally unappealing.

He heard Maitland over the intercom:

'The nav box is u/s and the D/F indicator. It'll have to be dead reckoning from now on.'

Hunting said:

'I've got news for you too. The clock's packed up and half the instruments are kaput, so I'm flying blind. It's up to you! D'you want to abandon and jump? Even if we maintain this height, whatever that may be, I won't be able to tell whether the Lanc's flying arse over tit or if we're hedge-hopping when things get ropey. Does anybody have a view?'

Barton said:

'We've got this far more or less in one piece. Unlike Howells, I don't fancy being the Führer's guest. I say we press on regardless. After all, Maitland's supposed to be King of the Navigators' Union and a wizard at taking a star fix. I'm here because I fancied living dangerously.'

Hunting said:

'What about you, Collins? Are the fuel gauges u/s?'

'Not so far as I can tell.' Collins smeared away the carbon deposit, left by the fire, off the instrument panel dials with the black silk fingers of his electrically heated glove. 'The pressure seems to have dropped in number three starboard, but the coolant seems O.K. You should be able to aviate us out of this one. If you get browned off, I'll give it a bash.'

'O.K. then.'

Fairclough said faintly:

'The RDF's working if anyone wants to know, and the Monica's got enough juice to keep us informed as to the whereabouts of the Luftwaffe.'

'That's á bonus. You all right, Sergeant?'

'I'm still recovering the use of my hands, but don't worry. I'm not reporting sick at this stage.'

'O.K. Now listen, Maitland and Collins, we have Night-fighter trouble, you'll have to climb into the empty dust-bins.'

Maitland said moodily:

'I've only seen the outside of a gun-turret.'

'Not to worry about that,' Barton interrupted. 'Being a gunner's the next technical grade up from A. C. Plonk. There are eight simple operations after you've strapped yourself in. I'll spell it out for you when it happens.'

'O.K.,' said Hunting. 'Professor, you better dream up a course. I want to cross the Rhine south of Luxembourg so we don't start waltzing all over the hills.'

'That's not going to be too easy. Due west from the Friedberg marker should take you to Rheims. That is, once we're over the Drachenwald. For the moment you better steer 265 magnetic and gain all the height you can.'

'What can you tell me about the Drachenwald?'

'Only what I can remember. It builds up to seven thousand feet and there's a castle on top.'

For the return they would have to cross the Drachenwald unless they turned south-west to skirt the flak defences beside the corridor between Emsdorf and Koblenz.

The reason why Maitland had some of the details in his mind was that he had marked the Drachenwald Schloss as his first fix at the start of his planned route back. The track he had now proposed would take them on a parallel, but slowly divergent course away from the returning Main Force track, once they had crossed the Drachenwald.

As he banked, Hunting said tersely:

'It's not just marked on the route map either.'

The way across the long, rising hump of the Drachenwald was clearly indicated by a broad corridor of brightly burning incendiaries that had set the pine forest alight, a finger of forest fire running up the long, smooth gradient.

'Any idea what's on the other side?'

'It's as flat as the home stretch on the Epsom downs, give or take a pimple or two.'

Hunting tried to estimate their height, after the long side-slip over Emsdorf. Was it a thousand, fifteen hundred or two thousand feet? At least it should not be too difficult to fly up a hillside lit by the fires that had resulted from the dumping of hundreds of burning incendiaries.

Barton said over the intercom:

'Looks as though the rabbits have been letting off their fireworks ahead of us.'

He spoke, now, with the near-confidence of a veteran. At least P for Peter had dropped its bombs on the target instead of simply jettisoning them.

12

Snappers

Hänsel and Gretel had been late arrivals at Beacon Ida, because Krasnatsky had deliberately reduced speed to make quite sure that he would not miss Lange at the Beacon. This consisted of two Peilkraftwagen A (Kfz 61) trucks stationed under camouflage netting in a wood outside the village of Beidenheim, transmitting on a prearranged frequency.

Hogel, Krasnatsky's operator, had spent the time testing the Flensburg and had picked up three passing contacts, which the Major had resignedly ordered him not to follow up. However, in each case the signal that Hogel had received on his cathode had been in the form of a cross, without any oscillation on the upper vertical arm.

The two Me-110s were nevertheless the first of the defending Nightfighters to engage the bomber stream at this point since Brown Bear's umbrella order had been countermanded by Reich Air Defence H.Q., Wannsee, west of Berlin. The Nightfighters had been dispatched on what soon turned out to be a wild-goose chase to Beacon Ludwig on the northern perimeter of the Ruhr.

As Krasnatsky circled Beacon Ida waiting for Lange, he nodded to the glare over Emsdorf and said:

'It is difficult to catch a fly in a darkened room, but easy if one turns on the light switch. What a pity there's nobody except us to do the job.'

Shortly afterwards Lange came up on the air and soon they established visual contact with each other.

Lange said:

'Some of the British crews have been off-loading in the Drachenwald. It should be a good spot. It looks like their turning-off point for the long journey home.'

Krasnatsky said:

'O.K., Fritz, I know where you mean. Don't let's waste any more time. With half the Nightfighters attacking Window contacts over Essen, the fighter controllers have really cocked it up tonight. It's time for a bit of action.'

He adjusted his eyepatch restlessly.

'I'll lead. Keep in visual contact until we have a target. O.K., Hogel, time to get busy with your new box of tricks.'

He started to turn towards the line of two thousand incendiaries, outside the target area, that blazed an unmistakable trail across the fields of Rheinhessen and up the Drachenwald, lighting up the sky with a steady glare for two miles.

This was the kind of action that Krasnatsky preferred, since he did not have to rely on the fighter controller or the erratic tantrums of his SN-2. The light from the burning forest made conditions near perfect for an attack.

As he eased the control column forward at ten thousand feet, his sharpened night vision quite clearly picked out the plan of a Lancaster, five thousand feet below him. For a reason he could not hope to understand, the bomber was making no attempt to assume a parallel and less obvious course away from the line of incendiaries in order to escape their glare.

He felt his left cheek twitch. From this angle the bloody thing looked like a travelling crucifix with over-extended arms.

'D'you see him, Fritz?' he said softly.

'It would be difficult not to. By the look of him it seems that he has problems.'

Hogel said excitedly:

'I'm beginning to pick him up on Flensburg. I'm getting the same signal, an oscillation at the top of the image. It must be the one that got away.'

Krasnatsky said:

'Let us end his problems for him. You only get one chance in this life. I shall come in from behind. You make a lateral pass in two minutes' time, Fritz, across his front. He will dive to starboard. If he tries to corkscrew, you can get him then, even if I don't, and in any case I'll be waiting for him at the top of his next climb.'

'I know exactly what you mean.'

Krasnatsky and Lange were used to working as a team so that, apart from agreeing the direction from which the attack should take place, orders were largely superfluous.

'We mustn't waste any more time. Judging from the fires in Emsdorf, the raid is almost over. They wouldn't stay longer than about thirty minutes. I want to get back upstairs to twenty thousand, once we've disposed of this straggler.'

Lange said thickly:

'Murdering swine.'

Krasnatsky made no further comment, disliking the eruption of any emotion which could disturb the precise and delicate calculation of a successful interception.

'We'll go off and hunt him now. Once you've reached position, give me a red flare. They'll notice that all right, but they won't figure on Hänsel picking up pebbles behind them. We'll still have Flensburg, if they run off to hide in the shadows.'

'I'll shoot a red radish in two minutes.'

Flight Sergeant Fairclough put down the processed-cheese sandwich on the wireless operator's table and, carefully rescrewing the thermos cap of his coffee flask, stowed it in the rack to his left. Then he said:

'I'm picking up something on Monica.'

The atmosphere in the aircraft immediately became electric.

Hunting said:

'If that wasn't all we needed. O.K., Maitland and Collins, you better man the turrets.'

Maitland tiptoed over McIndoe's bloody parachute canopy, swinging back the seat cushion of the upper-turret seat before hoisting himself in and adjusting the sliding block. He tried not to think of what had happened to McIndoe.

As he plugged in the intercom, he heard Barton say urgently:

'Switch on your gloves and oxygen and tape up your safety belt. O.K.?'

'O.K.'

'Now disengage the hand rotation gear on your left. Got it?'

'Yes.'

'Cock the guns and set them to "Fire".'

Maitland pulled back the cocking handles and moved the switch from 'Safe'.

'O.K.'

'Now turn the master firing switch at the top right of the panel.'

'Right.'

'Now turn on the sight switch. All you have to do now is push one of the two levers down on each side of you to traverse right or left. The tit on top of each works each gun.'

'I see,' said Maitland doubtfully. The night sky was luminous with the glare of flaming incendiaries but it still seemed dark and hostile to him after the cosy privacy of the navigator's compartment. He fought back a wave of rising fear.

'Aim three fingers off the nose if anything comes at you, but go easy on ammo. You've only two thousand rounds to play with and you could loose those off in four minutes if you tried really hard.'

Fairclough said:

'Now there are two signals.'

'What direction?' Hunting asked.

At that moment a red flare flashed into the sky a mile to starboard.

'Over there at four o'clock! Over there!' Collins shouted excitedly.

'The other's bound to be creeping up our arse,' Fairclough said.

Hunting began to turn to port while still trying to keep within sight of the line of flaming incendiaries that had set the woods ablaze on the slope of the Drachenwald. At the same time he brought up the throttles by two notches. Height, they must gain height.

'There it is, by the flare!' Collins shouted again. 'A two-engined job.'

Hunting said, desperately concentrating to retain control of the Lancaster's attitude:

'Then it's up to you and Maitland to see the bugger off.'

Maitland slowly swung the turret to starboard past the interrupter and depressed the guns. He could see nothing as yet because his eyes had not adjusted to night vision. Inside he felt the same feeling of careful calculation he got when he was working out a difficult fix except that now nothing was certain.

Collins said:

'The Snapper's closing in to starboard. In a moment he'll make a pass.'

Maitland saw the dappled white-and-grey shadow with its projecting radar antenna hover towards them behind a bursting spray of cannon fire and tracer. As a reflex, he depressed the firing triggers of his Brownings and tracer arced haphazardly away before plunging into the darkness.

'Not yet, you clot!' Collins shouted. 'Let him come in.'

Then he was interrupted by Barton:

'I see the other bastard. For Christ's sake climb, Cap!'

Barton waited for what seemed an eternity as the range closed to three hundred yards, before realizing that the second Nightfighter pilot had throttled back to maintain the same speed as the Lancaster. Barton sucked in his cheeks and waited. He had ten thousand rounds to play with: 1900 in each ammunition box and 2,400 on the ducts that ran through the rear fuselage from the upper turret. He no longer felt sick, waiting for the attack, crouched tensely behind the insubstantial armour plate, awaiting his chance to put a burst in on the enemy Nightfighter's props.

Maitland shouted:

'It's in close again!'

Hunting, hardly taking into account the rising gradient ahead, instinctively put the stick forward and the Lancaster began to dive.

'I wish we could lose these bloody incendiaries.'

Collins swung his Frazer Nash turret round and put in a burst at the source of the cannon shells, as the Me-110 side-slipped wildly beside them in an effort to bring its guns to bear on the target. Then it had vanished.

Collins shouted:

'Gone to ground!'

'Shut up, shut up, damn you!' Fairclough shouted.

Barton elevated his guns to maximum as the second insect-like white shadow skimmed over them, but it was impossible to get a shot in.

'Some bloody hopes.'

Dry-mouthed, Hunting pulled back the stick, fearful of the angle of the hillside below, for any second they might plough into the slope of the dark pine forests and he had no idea whether the aircraft would respond in time. He increased the throttles to maximum, pushing the engines until he guessed that they were climbing at just under two hundred miles an hour. He saw the shadow of the Lancaster flicker across a forest ride, lit by the glare of burning bombs. Suddenly ahead there was a ridge and the square oblong of the castle.

Fairclough said, as Lancaster left the glow of the incendiaries:

'Now they're both to starboard.'

Krasnatsky's left cheek twitched in the darkness.

'That time the hills almost did the job for us. Next time take them from the front, Gretel. Don't use a flare. Just tell me when you're starting your pass.'

He heard Lange's voice through the sidetone.

'We'll get them if it kills me.'

Krasnatsky looked over his shoulder to Hogel and said slowly:

'Are you picking up a signal on the Flensburg?'

The wireless operator was crouched across the three

dead cathodes of the Lichtenstein, tuning the Flensburg set:

'I'm still picking up that oscillation.'

From the information that Maitland had given him, Hunting knew that P for Peter must be at eight thousand feet as they flew past the Drachenwald Schloss. Now, provided he kept on course, flying straight and level, from that point on they should be well above the undulating land mass that stretched due west from the German frontier to the Channel. Assuming, of course, that they met with no further attacks.

Now that they were hidden by the welcome darkness away from the burning bombs and there was only the red and yellow glare behind to remind him of the burning city, Hunting suddenly felt more confident. At eight thousand feet there was at least some margin if they were forced to dive again.

Fairclough said over the intercom:

'Here they are again.'

In a moment Hunting lost his feeling of complacency.

'What direction?'

'Forward and aft. The signal's stronger forward.'

Maitland interrupted:

'Keep to the heading I gave you, Cap. There are still hills to the north until we're into France.'

'What about the wind?'

'We've left the weather front behind, but there's the Thal wind in the Rhine valley, but nothing likely to bother us at the present height. I'll try and work a correction once we're rid of the Luftwaffe so we don't get too close to Paris. That carries a five star rating in the Michelin flak guide.'

'Belt up, will you?' shouted Barton. 'We're being attacked. Didn't you hear?'

'We'll cross that bridge when we come to it.'

'Yeah,' Collins joined in. 'Just stick to the job in hand.

Keep your eyes peeled for the Crickets.'

In the forward turret, Collins hunched himself over his guns with a growing feeling of anticipation.

The sense of failure and anti-climax he had felt as a result of the incident over the bomb heater-switch had largely evaporated, but he still had the urge to prove himself to the rest of the crew in some way. It was a very bad show for a pilot officer to put up that kind of black in the middle of a crew of sergeants on their first operation. He remembered the leadership training course which had emphasized that it was only possible to be accepted as leader by example.

What made it altogether worse was that he could not be entirely certain whether his oversight was not due to some kind of subconscious funk. Although he was not generally given to introspection, he tried to relive the emotions he had experienced as he lay on the air bomber's couch, his attention divided between the rhythmic salvos of flak and the crossline of the Mark XIV bombsight as it moved slowly towards the aiming point and the smoke and flames which hid Emsdorf.

In the end, he decided that these moments in no way constituted a test of his personal courage for he had felt no fear that he could recall. It seemed like a dream where one opened a bottle of Scotch only to find that it contained water.

A better test now lay ahead with the renewed Night-fighter attack. If Fairclough's prediction was correct, he would soon be face to face with a target that would not only fight back, but was intent on destroying them. He was sure that the performance he was about to put up would certainly earn him the respect of the crew and remove the ambiguity that surrounded his position as an officer.

Fairclough said:

'They're closing in. You should have a visual to your front over the next few seconds.'

In his nervousness, Maitland gripped the starboard traverse, swinging the upper turret back and away from the target towards the rear quarter of the Lancaster. He stopped the turret and clumsily reversed direction.

Collins said:

'Target coming up at bang on twelve o'clock.'

At least that is what he believed, since he caught a vague movement in the shadows ahead of him, as he peered through his sight, overcome with the realization that he was now in total command of the situation, his hands poised waiting over the triggers of his twin Brownings, to make certain of a kill at the first burst.

Gretel's approach was, however, at a slight angle to the track of the Lancaster, and while Maitland wildly moved his turret to and fro to locate the target, he anticipated the path of the Nightfighter accidentally so that when he gripped the triggers instead of the master valve control levers, that operated the traverse, as he had intended, his twin Brownings spat a prolonged burst of one hundred and eighteen .303 rounds into the insect-like nose of the Messerschmitt 110, shattering the SN-2 aerials, buckling the port prop and binding the transmission unit of the port Daimler-Benz engine.

Gretel immediately side-slipped below the Lancaster, the side-slip uncontrolled and involuntary, since Leutnant Lange was blinded by a gush of hot engine oil from a severed oil pressure lead, while, a second later, four .303 rounds shattered his lower jaw, lodging in his neck and chest cavity.

As he died, the stick flopped loosely from his fingers and the port engine seized and the wing dropped, while the starboard engine, still at full revolutions, tore into the air and twisted the Me-110 into a spin.

As Emsdorf and the Drachenwald distantly revolved at an accelerating rate, the radio operator, who had survived Maitland's fortuitous attack, tried desperately to heave Lange to one side. It was a futile attempt since the Leutnant was strapped in by his safety belt and his feet were now fully jammed in the elevator shoes. All he succeeded in doing was to push the pilot's body forward, so that it slumped over the control column, making the aircraft assume an almost vertical attitude as it continued to spin.

Five seconds later Gretel struck the western slope of the Drachenwald at a velocity of three hundred and seventy-seven miles an hour, the fuselage impacting into the hill-side to a depth of twenty feet. The wings were ripped off as the aircraft struck the ground and the wing-tanks exploded, sending up a transitory flash through the night as four hundred and fifteen gallons of high octane fuel spontaneously ignited and kindled a glowing beacon and the tail plane and rear fuselage caught fire in their turn.

Hunting said:

'You earned your A.G. badge tonight all right, Professor.'

'I don't know how I did it,' Maitland answered with a hint of triumph in his voice.

'Isn't he a modest lad!' Fairclough commented. 'And to think that they taught him to map read as well.'

Barton said:

'He can take over from me any time.'

Then Fairclough said:

'Well, chaps, you'll be pleased to hear that I'm losing the signal on Monica. The other sod's pushed off to look for his friend.'

Hunting said:

'He'll be lucky if he finds him. Beginner's luck maybe, but at least we'll be credited with a kill.'

Collins' belated congratulations sounded cold and stilted in contrast:

'Wizard show, Maitland. I always knew you had it in you. You got it in first. I was just about to press the tit myself.'

Barton said:

'Yeah, well, it's thanks to Maitland that both the buggers are off our backs.'

Hunting nursed P for Peter back on track in a state of near euphoria, wondering how far south they had drifted. Feeling a new and different turbulence across the aircraft as he returned to the compass bearing Maitland had originally given him, he put it down to a valley wind they were encountering as they crossed the Rhine. In a few minutes they should be in France.

'O.K., boys, back on your stations. Give me a fix, Professor, and come back and check the tanks for me, will you, Collins?'

Collins made his way slowly back out of the forward turret, resenting Hunting's brusque tone. The truth of the matter was that his pride had been wounded and his confidence undermined by Maitland's destruction of the Me-110. He had lost the opportunity of matching his nerve and skill in the private duel he had arranged in his mind with the attacking Nightfighter, now that the pedantic and methodical Maitland had beaten him to it by accident.

He checked the tanks and irritably passed on the information that the starboard number 3 was only reading ninty-seven gallons, which meant that it was only one third full.

'Can't you try and find out why? It could be important.'

Collins turned away in silent rage, but there was really nothing he could say.

Hunting was too busy to notice Collins' pique, since he was totally absorbed in keeping P for Peter flying at the correct attitude so that it would neither stall nor lose height. He glanced out of the side window from time to time in case he could catch a glimpse of the searchlight batteries around Metz, which would then give a rough indication of their position. As the Lancaster ploughed on through the darkness, Hunting's exhilaration after their victory began to evaporate, to be replaced by the uneasy feeling that after the Nightfighter attacks they were now thoroughly disorientated and even Maitland had no idea where they were.

13

Hänsel over the Drachenwald

Krasnatsky's night vision had been momentarily disturbed by the tracer fire ahead of him, and he had instinctively throttled back and moved his Nightfighter below and to port of the Lancaster. He recovered it quickly enough, but still could not fully accept the implications of what he then saw as Lange's aircraft plunged across his nose and under the British bomber, spurts of flame jetting from the random machine-gun hits that ran the length of the port exhaust shroud.

As Gretel vanished into the darkness below him, Krasnatsky's attention was immediately divided between anxiety as to the fate of the Messerschmitt and the tempting target provided by the slowly disappearing Lancaster. However, there was no question in his own mind but that he must turn and follow Lange's falling aircraft in case there were parachutes.

'Hogel, have you a bearing on that British heavy?'

'256 magnetic.'

'Take a radio-fix. We'll be back as sure as the Reichsmarschall's potbelly.'

Underneath his apparent indifference, Krasnatsky was controlling an unfamiliar and desperate sense of panic. It was not possible that Lange with whom he had flown with hardly a break over the last three years should have been shot down in flames as a British victory. It had to be another narrow escape.

Krasnatsky banked, his left cheek twitching in the darkness, hoping against hope that Lange had not been hit and they had abandoned the aircraft in time. Then he remembered the R/T.

'What happened that time, Fritz?'

But when he switched to receive on Gretel's frequency,

a voice was monotonously droning on:

'At half-past six, on the morning of the nineteenth, first ascending and then going down by the Waldstätter Lake, we came to Fitznau ... from there by water to Gersau. At noon we were in the hotel ...'

Krasnatsky switched off the channel with a curse:

'The *Tommys* have jammed our frequency with Goethe,' Hogel said. 'It's from his Autobiography.'

'Shut up, damn you!'

Krasnatsky zoomed low over the dark woods of the Drachenwald in a tense and uneasy silence. Then his eye caught a sudden glare of light in the centre of which, leaning at a crazy angle, was the unmistakable glowing cruciform double rudder and pencil fuselage of a Nightfighter. The ground around it was consumed by gouts of leaping flame.

Even then the Major could not believe that it was Lange.

Then Hogel said in a matter of fact way:

'That can only be Gretel. There were no other Nightfighters.'

'Shut up, damn you!'

Krasnatsky's mind raced. Lange dead; bitterness increasing his usual restlessness.

'The rate they were going, there'd be no time to get out.'

Krasnatsky said:

'Shut up, Hogel. Now listen, Hogel. I'm getting that *Tommy*. D'you hear me?'

Finally overawed by the intensity in Krasnatsky's voice, Hogel swallowed and said:

'Yes, Herr Major.'

'I warn you, you've a busy night ahead. We're staying up until we shoot him down. I don't care how long it takes or if your eyeballs burst with staring at that damn blue cathode. But I'm going to get him. Don't you worry about that.'

'What about the controller?'

'Stuff the controller. A fine mess they've got us into tonight with that spoof to Beacon Ludwig. Anyway, how are we expected to communicate with all this Tommy jamming? No, Hogel, don't you worry about the controller.

Just get busy with the Flensburg.'

As he flew west, Krasnatsky suddenly realized that he did not care if he never flew again, so long as he could see the Lancaster plunging down and turning turtle in a sheet of flame. Apart from his long-standing debt, he owed that much to Lange and, like the Nordic Chief, the Leutnant should have a conquered enemy to accompany him to Valhalla that night. Not that Krasnatsky believed in such myths, he was far too practical a man for that. It simply somehow seemed appropriate.

What had happened was frequently the fate of young and inexperienced air-crew overconfident on their first half-dozen operations; invariably overestimating the vulnerability of the flying furniture-vans and at the same time underestimating their fire-power. He simply could not believe that the experienced Lange could have made a tactical error resulting in disaster; he could only have been the victim of some unforeseen accident. But then every death in the air battle was in a sense accidental. Unless you were killed outright, there was always the possibility of escape.

He glanced at the fuel gauges. With the reserve wing-tanks there would be almost enough to take him to Dover and back.

By now they had recrossed the dark western shoulder of the Drachenwald as Hogel swept the sky ahead with his Flensburg.

'Contact, I have a contact.'

'Is it that Lancaster?'

'How can I tell that, Herr Major? You credit me with supernatural powers.'

'You told me it gave off a special signal.'

'Then it's not that one,' Hogel said flatly. 'There's lots of trade, Herr Major. Won't another do?'

'I want that one, shithead. Get that into your thick skull once and for all, before you make me really lose my temper.'

'It could be anywhere, flying at 6,000 metres. That's where they usually try to get up to on the way back, for the cloud cover.'

Krasnatsky spoke slowly and distinctly, but now there was an edge to his voice:

'The one I'm interested in won't. It was in trouble. That's why they kept to the ground along that bomb line.'

'Sorry, Herr Major, I'm not a mind-reader. I only operate the radar.'

Krasnatsky controlled himself this time, realizing that without Hogel's co-operation he would get nowhere.

'All right, Hogel, don't worry. You just stick to your set. I'll do all the thinking that'll be needed tonight.'

Krasnatsky checked his altitude. After crossing the Drachenwald, the English Lancaster had maintained a height of eight thousand feet. If he was right, they were unlikely to climb any higher because of the difficulties on board.

'Give me a projected course of 256 magnetic from the Drachenwald Schloss.'

'Dead reckoning would take them to Rheims. After that he would have to change course to avoid Paris.'

'My guess is he'll make a north-west turn just south of Paris to avoid the flak and take the shortest route back home over the Channel.'

They continued along this track for fifteen minutes as Hogel strained at the Flensburg plot, sweeping the sky ahead and picking up a variety of signals.

Of course Krasnatsky had had no business to leave his sector outside the jurisdiction of the Nightfighter controller, just to gratify the obsession to avenge the death of his friend, but Hogel wasn't going to argue with him about it, in his present mood.

Suddenly the operator caught and held a momentary flicker on the Flensburg set, a fin-like oscillation moving across the top of the cathode. The signal came from a considerable distance to the south-west.

'My guess is that they've been taken there by the drift. They're probably being looked over right now by the fighter boys at St Dizier.'

'I hope to God you're wrong. This has developed into something personal.'

14

Flying Blind

After the battle Maitland fell into a trough of depression and anticlimax. It took some minutes for him to take in the implications of the devastation inside the navigator's compartment, and realizing the full extent of the damage offended first of all his sense of order.

The black curtains hung in charred ribbons. The paint on his table had bubbled and flaked with the heat of the fires and was now littered with pieces of glass from the shattered cathode of the nav box.

Glass and metal fragments crunched under his flying boots as he searched in vain for the remnants of his carefully marked roll of maps. The fire had destroyed them all except for a section showing Denmark and another the Isle of Wight. He carefully put these to one side as he retrieved his navigator's log. That at least had escaped serious damage.

Otherwise, all that remained intact was the P-type compass and the bubble sextant.

As he tried to reduce the chaos which surrounded him to some kind of order, the slogan of the navigator's union repeated itself subconsciously: 'Man is not lost ... Man is not lost ...' with a persistent rhythmic irrelevance.

The last remnants of elation finally evaporated with the sombre realization that, with what equipment he now had left at his disposal, it would be impossible to navigate effectively. This unpalatable fact was rubbed in by what he could see, or rather not see, through the window of his curtainless compartment. Beyond there was nothing except unrelieved blackness without even a solitary searchlight beam to indicate the presence of a city, or a reflection on a river, or a road or railway line.

'Where are we, Professor?'

'I haven't a clue. I have no way of telling.'

Maitland suddenly felt himself totally indifferent. All he wanted to do was sit there until they hit a mountain or ditched in the Channel. It was bad enough to have to make decisions which could affect all of them, when it was possible to acquire the necessary information with some degree of certainty, but without it, it was out of the question. He began to arrange his compass rose and circular protractor on the bare, flame-scorched table.

'Sorry, can't help.'

'Well, presumably we're still over Europe?'

'I couldn't even guarantee that. All the maps are useless. In fact, there aren't any.'

'That won't get us very far.'

'We can keep on flying until we're out of fuel.'

Maitland sat doggedly at his station, removing pieces of broken glass from the fascia of the Gee-equipment. It really was up to Hunting now. His guess was as good as his.

Hunting said:

'What does your log-book say?'

'Nothing we don't all know about.'

'You must have noted our last position and speed and so on.'

'Yes and also the fact that we fought off two very determined Nightfighter attacks.'

'Well?'

'Well what?' Maitland said irritably.

'You do want to finish the operation, write it up, I mean. It wouldn't look very good if there wasn't a complete record.'

Maitland fidgeted with the log, studying the entries he had made in his precise clerical hand. What Hunting said was true. There was something incomplete about the log as it was. If they were shot down or something, a Board of Inquiry might consider that in itself to be a reasonable excuse for not having the entries fully up to date. But if they did by some miracle get back and it was left in its present state ...

'It wouldn't be professional.'

Barton said:

'What the hell are you on about, Maitland? Be a good bloke and just find out where we are.'

'I have every intention of doing so,' Maitland said coldly.

Hunting said:

'How about an astrofix?'

'What's the good of an astrofix without a map to plot it on?'

'I've got a pocket diary,' Collins said. 'There's a map of Europe in the back of that.'

Hunting said:

'We can work that one out while you're sorting the problem. At least you can enter the bearing and time in the log.'

'O.K., Cap. I'll take a shufti through the dome.'

After he had removed the bubble sextant from its padded case, grateful for the fact that it had escaped any obvious damage, Maitland made his way back to the astrodome, a perspex-moulded hemisphere on top of the canopy behind the wireless operator's station. After carefully cleaning the carbon deposit from its inner surface with a piece of McIndoe's parachute, Maitland took up position inside it, grateful that there was, at least, no cloud to speak of.

The stars flickered brilliantly down through the soft darkness high above, in contrast to the hostile blackout covering the Earth below. He began to feel better as he recognized the great navigational constellations of the Plough, the Sickle, Pegasus and Orion. It was strange to feel so suddenly at peace.

Turning his watch to the inside of his left wrist, he held the bubble sextant steadily in both hands, putting it to his eye in the direction of the Plough. Then he rotated the sextant mirrors until the reflected image of Arcturus coincided with the bubble, repeating the operation five times, before depressing the clutch and returning the fine adjustment counter-clockwise to zero. When he noted the time he had taken to shoot the star, he took down the averaged-out reading for the six star shots from the tens scale, and the totalizer degree and minute drums. The angle of altitude was 147 degrees, 45 minutes. He repeated the same process twice more, this time shooting Dubhe and Spica at the zenith and nadir of the Plough, noting their angle of altitude in relation to the moving plane of the Earth as being 195 degrees and 161 degrees and 14 minutes respectively.

When he walked slowly past Fairclough at the wireless operator's station, he was smiling below his oxygen mask. He returned to the navigator's compartment to plot the coincidence of the three arcs in relation to the rotation of the Earth. Since these ellipses were predicted, it would then be possible to plot latitude and longitude using the celestial tables.

The operation had taken several minutes and Hunting was getting anxious.

'O.K., Prof? Worked out anything yet?'

'I've got a fix, unconfirmed. Latitude 48°, 47 North. Longitude 06°, 05 East. Averaged-out at seven minutes ago on an estimated track of 265 magnetic. I've no precise idea of drift, although I should estimate that twenty-five minutes back from Emsdorf we could be well over a hundred miles off course.'

'What precisely does all that mean in plain language, Professor? Where are we on the map?'

'I can tell you that when you've found me one. I don't have any maps. They were all ruined by the flak. I told you that.'

Fairclough said:

'McIndoe's got a map.'

Collins said:

'He won't need it where he's gone.' But nobody laughed.

'What kind of map?' Barton asked. 'The Dominion of Canada?'

'Western Europe printed on silk,' Fairclough said. 'They have them in most escape kits. He was wearing his as a scarf under his battledress blouse.'

Collins tried again:

'But seriously, it'll have to be returned to the Committee of Adjustment.'

Barton said:

'They'll be sealing all our rooms tomorrow, if we don't stop frigging about.'

Barton kept his intercom switched through, so they all heard the rattle of his twin double-Brownings as he edgily fired them off into the night, to ensure that the mechanism had not seized up with frost.

Fairclough removed the scarf from the dead man and handed it to Maitland. The map, although heavily creased and bloodstained in the bottom left-hand corner, was nevertheless quite readable when the navigator stretched it over his table, clipping it on either side with four spring clips. He made a rapid measurement.

'Five miles south of Mirecourt.'

'A very suitable name. Where the hell is it?'

'Fifty miles south of Nancy.'

'Christ! That's miles off course. At that rate we'll end up in Switzerland. Are you sure, Professor?'

'As sure as it's possible to be without a visual fix.'

Collins said:

'You're quite sure we're not on a reciprocal, Cap, taking us all the way back to Emsdorf.'

Hunting didn't bother to answer and none of the others seemed to think it was very funny either.

'What's the fuel situation, Collins?'

'Just over nine fifty gallons. Could be worse. Number 3 starboard's still losing even though the tank's been cut out.'

'I don't like the sound of that much. Looks like we've been done by shrapnel.'

Maitland made a rapid calculation. Cruising at 155 mph would give them twelve hundred miles of flying. Without allowing for emergencies it would still be five hundred miles to Manston. There was also the factor of the apparently leaking tank.

However, there was, as yet no confirmation of the accuracy or otherwise of the navigator's fix. According to the silk map, they should cross the Marne south of Joinville, picking up the Seine canals and a lake just to the east of Troyes.

'See anything, Professor?'

'Damn all. You'll have to go lower.'

Only the aircraft's attitude against a faint glimmer from the Milky Way in the western quarter of the sky gave Hunting any indication that he was holding the Lancaster's nose above the horizon.

'You'll have to try a flare.'

'What, and have the Nightfighters on our backs? We're within spitting distance of St Dizier as it is.'

'I wish I could be so certain. We should be able to see the Paris defences soon if I'm right. But all we can see is damn all. Do we check position or don't we?'

'O.K., Maitland.'

'On D/R we should see the lake in three minutes.'

'O.K., Maitland. Fairclough, drop a flare.'

Fairclough went back from his station to the flare chute stowage. He fixed the chute extension in the duct at the centre of the fuselage floor and took one of the four-foot flares off the rack below the cabin light. Then he placed the flare in the chute, propeller up and with the catches on inside the extension tube, hooking the cord on the reel, at the end of the tube, to the middle of the propeller. Then he released the chute catch and, after the flare slid out, he rewound the cord.

Almost immediately they were aware of the incandescent candle that floated behind them, swinging to and fro under its canopy and broadcasting over a million candlepower across the countryside so that it even filtered into the fuselage cabin and cast shadows. Barton was blinded by the intensity of the light and could see nothing. Maitland peered through his window and shouted triumphantly:

'There's the lake.'

The visual sighting restored his confidence, justifying the long minutes he had painstakingly spent at work under the astrodome.

To the north, the navigator could just make out the silver-steel glimmer of the two tree-lined Seine canals that led into the lake.

'Troyes,' Maitland said. 'Now I can give you a course

correction.'

Hunting stretched out and altered the setting on the D/R compass after Maitland had hastily calculated the triangle of velocities which should establish the wind-speed and their drift.

'You better fly on 300 magnetic.'

'Where will that take us?'

'North-east of Paris. It means we should come out by Dieppe.'

Collins said:

'I'm beginning to see SLs[1] at eleven o'clock.'

'Those'll be the Paris defences.'

'D'you think they can hear us coming?'

Hunting shivered slightly. The operation seemed interminable, and he wondered if he would ever relax again as he constantly checked the revolution counters, listening for any fall-off in the throb of the engines which might indicate that they were approaching a stalling angle.

Then Fairclough said:

'You better tell me what to do, Cap. I've picked up another contact on Monica.'

15

Bois de Vincennes

Krasnatsky saw the glimmer of the parachute flare released twenty miles away as he extracted every available ounce of power from the twin 1150 Daimler-Benz engines. He calculated that they should have a visual sighting in five minutes.

Hogel said:

'They're turning north-east. Looks as though they're gong to cross Paris. What a circus!'

Krasnatsky said:

'That's only to be expected. The *Tommys* are as anxious

[1] Searchlights.

to put down their landing gear as I am to catch up with them.'

In different circumstances, Krasnatsky might almost have felt sorry for the limping and isolated bomber, but the outcome of the battle on the west side of the Drachenwald had changed all that.

Hogel said:

'Yes, they're definitely turning north-east. Their new course will practically take them along the Champs Elysées.'

Krasnatsky's right cheek twitched.

'That pilot needs his head examined. All right, Hogel. I'm following him in. I'd like to shoot him down before any flak batteries get lucky.'

Hogel was silent for a moment and then he said:

'Forgive me for saying so, Herr Major. But I understood that Paris was a prohibited zone.'

'Don't worry, Hogel, you'll live to tell your grandchildren all about it. The flak boys round here could only drop a cannonball on a soup plate by accident.'

Krasnatsky seemed overexcited and in a mood that Hogel had never seen before, equally exhilarated by the prospects of victory and of avenging the death of his friend Lange. The Major was almost laughing, now that they had caught up with the Lancaster once more.

'Besides, Hogel, it'll give you the chance to tour Paris by night, pick out all the landmarks you see on the picture postcards, the Eiffel Tower, Étoile and the Moulin Rouge. It'll be a unique experience, so make the best of it.'

Hogel was not totally convinced that Krasnatsky was behaving normally and was far from enthusiastic about the risky treat that the Major had in store for them, since he was well aware that Paris was protected by at least a hundred flak batteries, however unpractised the crews of German reservists and French volunteers were, compared with the battle-hardened veterans of the west Reich cities.

'As the Major wishes, but I feel it my duty to repeat that Air Sector Paris is a Luftwaffe-prohibited zone and that any aircraft passing over it is automatically designated as a target.'

'Maybe you should let the *Tommy* in on your secret. Anyway, if you're uneasy there's always the flare pistol, provided you know the correct signal for the day.'

Collins said:

'I hope you know what you're doing, Cap. It looks like we're going to be buying extra trouble.'

Hunting said wearily:

'It's quite clear they're tracking us on their radar. I take the view that the only chance we've currently got is to keep their minds otherwise engaged. It may be a ropey idea to fly across Paris in our state, but we won't be the only target if they follow. In any case they might duck out, and we could lose them once we get to the other side. If we're first out of the wings and get away with it the Frog gunners will probably have their eye in by then and bracket them more easily.'

As he finished speaking, the sky lit up in front of them as the searchlights of the western perimeter defences from Tremblay, Bobigny, Bois de Vincennes and Vitry-sur-Seine switched on, their combined batteries forming a curtain of wavering lights.

Hunting was blinded each time the Lancaster flicked through a searchlight beam, and the batteries started to swing together to form a cone. Increasing revolutions, he pushed the air-speed up to over two hundred miles an hour. The Lancaster passed through this outer barrier without incident and the searchlights flickered and trailed after him, throwing the Eiffel Tower into black silhouette. Now Hunting could see the city centre clearly lit from the reflected light off the cloud base. The radii of boulevards running off the Arc de Triomphe came into view, as P for Peter followed the Seine above the Quai d'Austerlitz, to the bend where the river curved west at Les Invalides.

Barton said:

'Light flak and plenty of it.'

The principle source of the barrage that now pursued

them was the two hundred and thirty-seven 25-mm French Hotchkiss cannon which were not radar-controlled. These were supported by sixteen Grosse Batterien, provided for the city's defence by Flakkommando West Frankreich, armed with 88-mm Flak 18s and 36s. However, since the nature of the intrusion was not immediately obvious, that night's duty officer was reluctant to order an all-out barrage to eliminate nothing more than a solitary British heavy which seemed to be flying in company with a De Havilland Mosquito. The reason for this was that the Flak Divisional Commander had very firm views on unnecessary ammunition wastage, as staff at every level were constantly being reminded.

Nevertheless, the duty officer authorized fire orders for the batteries of 25-mm Hotchkiss cannon grouped round the military fortress of Vincennes, which began to put up a barrage, averaging a hundred and seventy-five rounds per gun each minute. At first the flak groped above the aircraft at fifteen thousand feet.

When the aim improved, the Lancaster's wings juddered from the maelstrom caused by the turbulence of these exploding half-pound shells, as P for Peter passed over Neuilly, Colombes and Sartrouville before crossing once more into the neutral darkness to the north-west of Paris.

For a moment Hunting removed his aching hands from the control column, wondering whether he dared trust the automatic pilot when his own instruments had failed. In the end he decided against it, since it was impossible to tell what damage it might have sustained over Emsdorf and, in any case, they were still at risk from Nightfighter attack.

Barton said:

'Well, for once that was surprisingly simple. I wonder what happened to the Luftwaffe.'

Looking back from the rear gun-turret, the Australian could see that the western defences were already damping down their searchlights; but there was no sign of any enemy Nightfighter against the grey mists that covered the rest of the city. The countryside below, with its scattering of great forests, had already assumed a lunar and impersonal anonymity.

By this time Krasnatsky, five miles behind the Lancaster and halfway across Paris, almost regretted his decision to follow in the track of the heavy bomber as Hänsel began to be tossed from side to side as the flak gunners' aim improved.

'God Almighty!' shouted Krasnatsky, after passing through a particularly turbulent area. 'Can't you give them the signal for the night?'

'I've done it twice,' Hogel said sullenly. 'Clearly they're not impressed. They must know perfectly well that the British master bombers and pathfinders carry a full supply of signal flares and other fireworks to confuse the defences. To them we're just another hostile aircraft.'

'Did you check it in the book?'

'Yes, Herr Major. Red ... white ... green.'

Suddenly the alloy skin forward of the canopy was pock-marked by a flickering shower of splinters that tore the metal-like cloth. At the same time, Krasnatsky felt a sudden and dangerously menacing deceleration and the Me-110's nose reared up. Glancing to one side, he saw that the wing flaps were extending while the panel switch had mysteriously moved to 'Landing Position.' Turning back the switch to 'Normal Flight', he saw the flaps begin to retract with some relief.

Hogel did not notice what had been going on, since a splinter had also penetrated the bullet-proof Perspex of the canopy and passed through the flesh of his right hand, just above the junction of his thumb and index finger. This meant that it was now agony for him to tune the Flensburg set. He did not complain openly at first, however, merely mouthing obscenities at the Major's back in the darkness. At last he could restrain himself no longer and said:

'Begging your pardon, Herr Major, but do you reckon that we've got any chance of getting back now, or would you like me to think about opening the Air Sea Rescue Channel?'

Krasnatsky stiffened.

'Don't say you've lost the target on the Flensburg?'

'Not exactly, but I do have this little cut from the flak that doesn't help me much, but your Lancaster's on a heading of 345 and it won't be long now before we hit the coast.'

Krasnatsky increased throttle, but found that, as soon as the aircraft exceeded an airspeed of 190 miles an hour, the hydraulics began to vibrate as the flaps extended to drop into position at the back of the wings.

This time Hogel noticed it too and was clearly unimpressed by the sudden and unnerving behaviour of the aircraft's flight control surfaces.

After one or two risky experiments, Krasnatsky settled down to a different kind of pursuit as the Me-110, now only marginally exceeding the speed of the heavy bomber, crept forward on the track of the Lancaster, while Hogel no longer attempted to conceal his intense disapproval of the risks that Krasnatsky was running.

16

Channel Crossing

Maitland said over the intercom:

'I've just had a visual fix on Pontoise, Cap. I reckon that more or less wraps it up for the moment. We're almost home and dry.'

The navigator carefully recorded the entry in his log before closing the book and neatly arranging it beside the instruments that covered Poland on McIndoe's silk map of Europe.

He had given Hunting a course of 355, which, allowing for drift, should take them up the narrow corridor north from Paris, with Evreux and Rouen to the west and Beauvais to the north-east. This should bring them to the coast between Dieppe and Abbeville without the need for another fix.

Now that they had crossed Paris it really seemed rather simple and there was very little more for him to do.

Fairclough said over the intercom:

'Are you going to make a blind landing when we cross the Channel?'

'It's pretty definite unless you can fix the R/T.'

'I'm not a radio/mech.'

'Haven't you got a box of spare valves? I don't want to ditch unless I have to. But you must lay on something because we'll never make it unless we can get through to Darky.'

Darky was the emergency service that guided distressed aircraft in to an emergency landing on the nearest suitable airfield.

Fairclough said reluctantly:

'I suppose I can have a bash. I'll certainly fit new anodes for a start, but I can't begin to say what kind of a mess the circuits are in.'

Hunting fought back the resentment he felt that, while the rest of the crew was starting to relax and take things easy, he still had to fly on through the darkness, straining into the night ahead, sensitive to every change in the aircraft's attitude.

At last he said:

'O.K., everybody, but we're not at Dispersals yet by a long chalk, and don't any of you forget it! Have you still got that contact, Fairclough?'

Fairclough, unscrewing the top of his thermos, did not answer immediately.

'I've still got some kind of contact, but I don't understand it. It seems to be trailing. If it was a Nightfighter, it should be keeping the gunners busy by now. It's at extreme range, but there it stays.'

'Just let me know if it starts to close in.'

Collins said:

'I'm glad we've got a moment or two to restore our

shattered nerves, but what happens when the coast comes up?'

'We cross it, of course. What else?'

Hunting wished that Collins had not asked that particular question, or any other, come to that. By doing so, he was anticipating another crisis. For a moment he considered whether he should not ask Collins to take over the controls, but then he knew that the officer was an indifferent pilot and they would all probably regret it if he attempted to fly by night without instruments.

'Yes, Cap, but it's the Luftwaffe primary Nightfighter and flak belt. You remember what happened when we came in?'

'Only too well.'

Collins said:

'Why don't you go down to zero feet? That way you'll fox their radar.'

Hunting said wearily:

'There are no instruments, or had you forgotten?'

'Well, in my view, they're hardly necessary. It's light enough outside to fly and see where you're going.'

For a moment Hunting felt inclined to vent his tired frustration on Collins, until he realized that maybe he was sitting too close to the problem and that what Collins said might even be right. Outside the canopy, Hunting saw that the moon had now risen, fitfully lighting up the landscape they were flying over.

'What happens if we run into ground fog at the coast?'

'The only thing that's certain at the coast is the flak.'

The more he thought about it, the more the idea appealed to Hunting. By dropping down as close as he dared, he might also eliminate whatever radar pulse the pursuing Nightfighter was picking up from the Lancaster. However, in his present state of mind he found it impossible to give Collins the credit for his suggestion. He eased the control column forward so that the Lancaster began to swoop down towards the darkness of the Norman countryside.

'I'm losing them,' Hogel said with an air of finality. 'Isn't it time we went home or landed somewhere? If I raise Abbeville, they can put up a shroud and switch on the flare-path for us.'

Krasnatsky was silent for a moment before replying, his back hunched intensely as he strained his night vision in vain for a sight of the Lancaster somewhere out there ahead. The Lancaster he had promised himself he would shoot down to make up for Fritz.

'You don't understand, Hogel, not one little bit.'

'No, Herr Major, I can't say I do.'

'Well, if you can't, don't bother to try. Just shut up and tell me their latest heading.'

'It has to be Dieppe, Herr Major. They're not going to risk flying the length of the West Wall.'

Krasnatsky made no attempt to increase throttle as the Me-110's engines ploughed into the night, under stress from the unusual dynamic load the constant slow running imposed on them.

'They must have gone hedge-hopping to get through the coastal defences. We're bound to re-establish the contact once they're over the Channel. Just keep your eyes glued to that cathode.'

Once Hunting was flying at what he estimated was a thousand feet, he found it was possible to fly with the nose of the Lancaster just above the horizon line, which was lit by the primary searchlight belts that hung and flickered like distant lightning away to the north.

However, the sergeant pilot throttled back to a hundred and sixty-five because he was afraid of insufficient margin, should he be faced with a sudden obstacle, and also because he had been flying the Lancaster constantly for over six hours under continuous stress. This, apart from the variations in altitude that they had all experienced, had depleted his adrenalin supply to such a degree that, as he flew on, he felt himself being overcome by wave after wave of sleep.

With his usual objectivity the sergeant pilot found this an extraordinary situation, since at one moment he was concentrating on half a dozen factors that concerned the safety of the aircraft, while at the next he had to pull himself back from falling into the soft darkness below. However, when he relaxed his grip on the control column, it began to edge forward, altering the aircraft's attitude almost imperceptibly. This change immediately returned him to full consciousness and control once more, but it was a constant and alarming inner battle.

Under these conditions he felt it impossible to do anything other than fly straight and level, even though he knew it would be better to weave, to disturb the aim of any alert flak battery or stalking Nightfighter.

Collins was the only crew member who suspected that anything was wrong.

'Won't you let me take over, Cap?'

'No thanks, I'm O.K.'

'You've been flying without a break since we started.'

'Well, that's all in the contract, isn't it?'

'Are you quite sure I can't take a turn, Cap? It's been a long hard night.'

He poured Hunting a cup of coffee.

'Why don't you relax and switch on George?'

'For all I know, the George is u/s, and besides, it's a clottish idea to switch on the automatic pilot at a thousand feet.'

Nevertheless he was grateful for the coffee, although he resented Collins and his bright ideas.

'You better check out the fuel situation.'

Hunting now discovered that he resented almost all the crew members, including the ones that were missing. He resented McIndoe for getting himself killed and Howells, the only other crew member who had been in any way competent to handle the Lancaster, for baling out and leaving him to grind on through the emergencies hour after hour without instruments.

The crew members who were left were in some ways

worse and he found that now he had to think carefully, very carefully before answering them when they came up on the intercom. He realized that invariably they would be presenting a new fact or asking a question, both of which would sooner or later involve him in making a decision, which he now felt he was no longer capable of making. The effort involved in any activity of that kind took too much out of him.

His involvement with and responsibility for the aircraft and the crew were constant and inescapable, whereas, when they flashed his station light urgently, it was only to tell him about some transitory problem they could usually deal with themselves if they applied common sense. His problem and responsibility would last as long as the operation and even beyond that, stretching into future time.

Now that he thought about it, Fairclough sounded patronizing and at the same time seemed only too glad to pass him any buck he didn't feel like handling, in spite of all his experience. Collins with his class-ridden Southern English accent and mannerisms dramatized everything like a schoolboy hero from the 'Boy's Own Paper'. Maitland was pedantic and obstinate, always having to be handled carefully with kid gloves, moody and sensitive. Even Barton had his drawbacks since Hunting was acutely suspicious of the effect that the Australian's bluntness could have on the other members of the crew.

If only he could go to sleep, he could discard all their personalities and problems, but if he did that, they would all of them be dead.

Having got so far, Hunting had no intention of dying. Other crews might generate a desperate, half-heroic, don't care, stiff upper lip confrontation with disaster that might even seem admirable, like the so-called 'Dunkirk spirit'. Hunting could only classify it and call it by what it was – failure. Death was the consequence of failure and the sergeant pilot had no intention of failing.

It was the nagging hatred of failure, in fact, which in the end stopped him from falling asleep at the controls, just as it had stopped him from venting his frustration on the other crew members. He was only too well aware, of course, that he and the aircraft relied on the others for protection, communication and navigation. Through some unfair pact they were all in one another's hands.

Fairclough said excitedly, his voice half-tinged with pride:

'I'm picking up a late programme on Radio Normandie.'

'That makes a change from what you've been picking up on Monica.'

'Don't worry. The Phantom Snapper's still there giving chase.'

'For Christ's sake don't make jokes about bloody Nightfighters,' Maitland said edgily.

Collins said:

'You'll get over it, Sergeant. They say the first victory's always the worst to come to grips with. It's a kind of nervous reflex action. You're doing fine.'

'That'll make the grass grow green in Texas, Collins,' Barton said. 'Why don't you tell him what he should feel after you've done it yourself?'

'O.K., O.K.,' Hunting said. 'That's enough of that. How are the fuel gauges reading?'

'Much the same as before, except you've used up another two hundred gallons.'

The searchlight beams ahead jerked backwards and forwards restlessly.

Maitland said:

'That's the coast all right. You better just keep on flying north until we strike Brighton.'

'Give it to me properly, please, Maitland.'

After a moment the navigator said:

'Heading 353 magnetic, Cap.'

Hunting stretched forward and set the new course on the D/R compass, shifting the rotating outer scale.

Because there was no artificial horizon, Hunting found himself forced to fly at the web of searchlight beams. As he did so, he lost more height, steering the Lancaster to the darkest patch of sky. He decided that it was time for the crew to do something for him for a change as he said over the intercom:

'Gunners, prang those searchlights. Just give them a burst as we fly over.'

He increased throttle on the last half-mile over the chalk cliffs.

17

Up and Under

Krasnatsky brought his Me-110 down to 1500 feet once they had crossed the Hindenburg Battery west of the Luftwaffe airfield at St Aubin, where Hogel had given the signal for the day. The wireless operator said sourly to Krasnatsky:

'They're asking me what the hell we think we're doing and who is our control.'

Krasnatsky was no longer interested in ground signals, now that they were over the Channel, as he concentrated once more on scanning the gloom ahead for the exhaust flames of the escaping Lancaster.

'We are engaged in the pursuit of a British heavy. I should have thought that was sufficiently obvious, or maybe they didn't pick it up on their Würzburgs.'

'That's what I told them. He was probably crossing pretty low.'

As the Me-110 swept over the sea, Krasnatsky waited tensely, as tensely as the time that he had waited for Rosa, the Viennese actress who had not responded to his overtures for political reasons, and so he had stood one night for three hours outside the Opera in the Kärntnerstrasse, waiting for her to come out. Of course he had succeeded with Rosa eventually. It had been nothing more than a question of honour, and now he felt no emotion other than regret for Lange's death. But that was not entirely true. As they had crossed Northern France, he had felt his inner restlessness growing with the pursuit, knowing that this was a prelude to the fighting madness that would overwhelm him once he caught sight of the Lancaster. At the same time this madness would be instantly absorbed in the cold calculation with which he always made an attack.

As he glanced down at his instrument panel, six red lights glowed at him like tigers' eyes, confirming that the six nose cannon were set to 'Fire', standing out brilliantly against the pale luminosity of the other instruments. Then Krasnatsky listened to the throb of the Daimler-Benz engines again and advanced the throttle slightly until the airspeed indicator hovered at just over 190 mph.

Hogel said resignedly:

'I have regained contact. I estimate that the target is flying on a heading of 350 magnetic and is about a mile ahead. Their altitude is about a thousand.'

'We're in luck. They did slow down then.'

'They must have done to cross the coast at that height.'

Fairclough was so busy adjusting the transmitter after he had located the Darky frequency on the receiver that he was not aware of the increasing, jagged signal on Monica. Until it was almost too late.

In fact, it was Barton who saw the Nightfighter first, as it began to make its attacking run, in the long classic swoop of the 'up and under' attack, dropping down momentarily below the Lancaster before climbing, at a slight angle, to bring the nose cannon to bear and hose the wings and rear fuselage with cannon fire.

'Nightfighter! Nightfighter! Coming up directly behind. Get the hell out of it, Cap!'

The next instant he was half aware of a sledge-hammer blow to his shoulder which threw him back against his safety harness, ramming his head at the metal entry port door. In the intervening half-second his hand instinctively groped for the starboard button, but the Browning fired wildly, there was insufficient depression and the tracer merely arced up and over the canopy of the attacking

Nightfighter.

At the same instant a cannon shell exploded at the back of the nacelle of the inner starboard Merlin, having sliced through the wing, ripping away the rear cowling, so that fragments penetrated the glycol heating jacket, supercharger impeller and driving gear, smashing the auxiliary drives. Four splinters also shattered the cylinder block, distorting the pistons in the two near-side cylinders. As a result the engine began to strain and judder on its mounting, as the crankshaft laboured to rotate and the rear half of the cylinder block began to glow red-hot. There was a flicker of flame from a severed fuel lead that almost instantly transformed the starboard inner engine into a roaring furnace.

Hunting was immediately aware of a power loss as the revolutions fell away, but he moved the throttles of the other three engines forward in compensation and the air-speed increased momentarily.

Once his night vision had returned Krasnatsky shouted:

'He's getting away from us! He's getting away! The bloody thing's indestructible.'

'This certainly doesn't seem to be our night.'

'He has to catch fire. I got his engine, I'm sure of it. Any moment his fuel tanks should blow.'

Nevertheless, Krasnatsky watched in dismay as the Lancaster began to creep jerkily away from the Me-110, while the Major kept on glancing down to where his air-speed indicator needle still wavered at 190 mph.

'It's no good. I've got to finish him. I must see it done.'

Hogel swallowed nervously.

'He has to slow down if you did hit an engine.'

'I hit everywhere. The rear-gunner must be dead. I can't understand it.'

Krasnatsky began to ease the throttles forward in preparation for another attack, millimetre by millimetre, as the air-speed indicator crept up from 190 to 195 to 200. The

Me-110 began to surge forward as the engines hummed gladly in response.

'I'll get him this time. The *coup de grâce*. Then off we go back to St Aubin.'

It was quite clear to Krasnatsky that every second was now taking him nearer the dark Lancaster silhouette.

He eased the throttles forward ... 205 ... 210. In fifteen seconds he would be able to rake the wings and fuselage again and put an end to it once and for all.

Krasnatsky's next salvo tore into the number one starboard tank, but the rest of the shots went wide. As his finger pressed the firing button and the red lights flickered off momentarily while the cannon reloaded, the Major felt a sudden inexplicable thumping which could not be the recoil. Then his heart missed a beat as he realized that the flaps had suddenly and totally extended.

The consequence of this, at the speed at which the Me-110 was now travelling, was complex. The first result of the additional strains placed on the flight surfaces was to rip off the end mounting of the port flap, parting it from the main wing so that it became an incongruous and unstable air-brake that twisted the aircraft over in a shuddering roll.

As he felt the sinister convulsions that now gripped the airframe, Hogel instinctively struck at his safety-harness release and pulled the cord of the rear canopy jettison. As he was thrown to the left, he was ejected, at the same time that, because of the new unacceptable dynamic forces, the Me-110's tail plane parted from the fuselage.

The aircraft now reared up like a hovering dragon-fly, but the twin screws could generate no horizontal lift. Krasnatsky pulled back at the stick, which had suddenly become limp in his hands, in a fruitless attempt to gain some kind of control over the elevators, as the Nightfighter hung at the zenith of a bizarre hammer stall, before spinning viciously to port.

Ten seconds later, Krasnatsky, still trying to work the non-existent elevators, found himself hanging upside-down from his straps, as the Me-110, halfway to its terminal velocity, plummeted towards the sea. As he did so, alone in his crazy world, he became aware of a flash of light surging along the trailing edge of the Lancaster's starboard wing, illuminating it in the form of a burning cross against the night sky.

'Victory. Total victory. Shot down in flames.'

Major Krasnatsky was still fumbling for the forward canopy release as the aircraft finally struck the water. The shock of its impact flung his body forward, impaling his stomach on the control column and splitting his skull open on the instrument panel. The uncontrollable forces released within the destroyed aircraft could do nothing more to Major Krasnatsky, however, since his heart failed at the precise moment that the nose of the Nightfighter struck the sea.

At the same time, the engines spluttered and died as the air-screws thrashed into the water at two hundred and forty miles an hour and the fuselage parted at the back of the canopy and the wings crumpled and snapped. All that was left of Hänsel was a floating landing-wheel still attached to its ripped-off strut, riding the swell in the centre of a dark patch of oil that fitfully gleamed and spread in the half moonlight.

Hunting suddenly became aware of the flames that licked along the starboard wing root from the red glow through the windows on either side of the flight engineer's panel. He immediately feathered the starboard inner engine, at the same time switching on the remote-control fire extinguishers. These, however, did not work since the electrical circuit which operated them had been disrupted by the flak-burst over Emsdorf.

The air-speed was already falling below a hundred and fifty miles an hour and, unless he achieved more power, the aircraft would be in danger of stalling. He could not tell precisely when this was likely to occur other than by the sound of the engines. However, he increased throttle to try and gain height as his senses strained to isolate the first tremor of tail-buffeting that would precede a stall.

As he worked at the controls, he realized the long-term consequences of the starboard inner failure; the compressor operating the wheel brakes could no longer function.

Gathering all his unsuspected reserves of mental and physical energy, he looked up to see Collins standing beside him, holding the crash axe. The pilot officer began to smash a hole in the side of the aircraft forward of the engineer's panel and over the wing.

'What's that supposed to be in aid of?' Hunting shouted.

'I'm going out there,' Collins shouted back against the roar of the engines. 'I'm going to put out that engine fire before the number one tank blows.'

'Don't be a B.F. You haven't a snowball in hell's chance.'

'There's not much bloody chance either way, since we're a flaming torch a thousand feet over the Channel. The chutes would never open in time and I don't fancy joining the Caterpillar Club. How the hell can you ditch safely without instruments?'

Collins continued to hack away at the alloy section, carefully avoiding the ducting, until at last the aluminium fell away, hanging momentarily against the angry red wing-fire before it was whipped off by the slipstream.

Collins then turned and said:

'You better start jettisoning that number one tank.'

Hunting nodded and reached for the jettison control to the left of his seat, which would drain away the petrol from the damaged tank.

When he looked back again to where Collins had been standing, he saw that the pilot officer was now no longer alone. Fairclough had detached two silk shrouds from McIndoe's parachute and Collins was tying these to his waist, as he climbed out onto the brilliant light of the wing, a fire extinguisher pushed inside his battledress blouse.

For a moment he stood uncertainly, blown back by the slipstream, before lunging forward onto his stomach and working his way along the leading edge where he painfully extricated the fire extinguisher and began to spray carbon dioxide into the jagged cannon holes at the back of the nacelle where the metal glowed dull red. Meanwhile, flaming petrol continued to stream away from the punctured wing-tank, adding to the cascade of fire that fell away from the jettison valve at the trailing edge.

Sergeant Barton recovered consciousness, surrounded by a spider's web of shattered Perspex as a howling gale sucked into the rear turret past the drunkenly angled Brownings. He was immediately aware of the heavy, thudding pain in his left shoulder and, for a moment, hovered once more on the borderline of consciousness as pain screamed through his useless left arm. He tried to switch on the intercom, before he realized that the lead had been torn away from the socket and was now nothing more than a useless piece of exposed wire, stripped of its plug. Then, as if he could only move in slow motion, he proceeded to unstrap his safety belt. Barton stood up, his head swimming, and clutched for support at the gun-mounting before forcing his way through the metal entry port doors, crawling over the tail-plane spar to the first-aid boxes besides the Elsan. As he moved, he could feel that the layers of clothing at his chest were stiff with blood, but when he looked down, he was unable to assess the extent of the wound. He opened the door of one of the first-aid boxes and removed a pre-loaded morphia syringe.

Hunting looked away from the bubbling paintwork on the fuselage wall beside the flight engineer's panel, where the dark green was turning brown and giving off little wisps of smoke. Then he said over the intercom:

'O.K., Professor, you can start dumping everything aft of the main spars – flares, ammo, the lot. I don't want the fire spreading inside as well as out.'

'What fire, Cap?'

'Didn't anybody tell you, Maitland? We've been pipped by a Nightfighter.'

'Oh, that.'

'Yes. Oh, that. Kindly extract fingers and go and do as you are told. Push everything you can down the flare-chute, but for God's sake don't set anything else off while you're about it.'

'O.K., Cap, got it.'

Mentally Hunting tried to calculate the weight of ten thousand rounds of .303 as he fought to keep the Lancaster's nose up. In the end he decided that it must come to something like two and a half thousand pounds, assuming that each round weighed four ounces with the belt links. Then there were the flares. They must be taken off their wall racks to avoid the possibility of sympathetic detonation, as the heat of the wing fire sweeping up against the starboard side of the fuselage was likely to set them off. The flares carried a magnesium powder charge and when they were set off they could generate a temperature in excess of 1200 degrees Fahrenheit.

Then he began to wonder how long it would take for the wing to catch fire. Aluminium began to burn at 1472 degrees, but petrol had a flashpoint of only a hundred. How long would it take for the slipstream to make up the difference and trigger off spontaneous combustion in the duralumin panels that covered the wing area?

Then he heard Maitland's voice over the intercom. He sounded panicky.

'It's Barton. He's been hit.'

'Hit? How badly hit?'

'Its hard to say, but his shoulder looks a mess. He's out cold, dosed himself up with morphia.'

'You better move him to the stretcher.'

'I'll do what I can, Cap. Stop the bleeding at any rate, put a shell dressing on. But I can't swear he'll survive if you ditch. I'd never be able to get him through the fuselage door in his present condition, let alone any of the upper escape hatches. His Mae West's a write-off and I don't suppose there's anything very much worth saving of the dinghy in the starboard wing. It must be cooked to ashes by now.'

From where he sat, Hunting glanced at the flames licking along the starboard wing root.

'That's a possibility that had quite slipped my mind. Anyway, get him back to the stretcher and then go and ditch the bloody flares.'

'I've done that, Cap. There's only the ammo now.'

'Good lad, don't be shy about heaving overboard anything that could explode. After this trip they'll have to give us a new aircraft.'

As he talked, Hunting instinctively held the correct flight angle, knowing that at any moment, if he lost control of the attitude and did not maintain the necessary speed, the Lancaster could scythe down through the darkness into the sea below. Disposing of a few hundred pounds of ironmongery was only likely to gain him a few feet in altitude but, more important, he did not want fire inside the aircraft.

A few moments later Maitland came back to him on the intercom:

'I've dumped all the ammo belts I could find in the boxes and under the upper turret. What else is there?'

'How's Barton?'

'Pretty ropey. He doesn't look too good and I don't think he'd ever get out. There's no sign of him coming round either.'

Hunting accepted the additional responsibility of a wounded and helpless crew member almost without thinking. If it had not been for Barton, he would never have dragged away from the pursuing Nightfighter, and by now they would probably all of them be dead or struggling to keep alive in the icy water of the Channel, those of them, that is, who were lucky enough to get that far.

'O.K., Professor. You better take a close look at Barton and see just how badly he's been hit. You should keep him warm and try and make him drink something hot. It sounds like he's in shock.'

'Wilco, Cap.'

Through the gap that Collins had slashed above the

wing root, it was possible for Hunting to see the pilot officer lying incongruously beside the feathering prop of the starboard inner. Now there were no more flames running back out of the holes the cannon shots had made in the skin of the nacelle.

For Collins the journey out along the wing, even although he was exposed to the blast of the slipstream, which could whip him off into the darkness below, gave him little to fear. It was really a climb of little technical difficulty, requiring at the outset more strength than skill. It is true, of course, that traversing the exposed rock faces of the Grochan and Clogwyn d'ur Arddu had little in common with a Lancaster wing, and that the conditions on those rock climbs would not exactly match the damp smooth surface of the leading edge without handholds, but it was near enough to be vaguely similar.

What was quite different and what caused every nerve in Collins' legs to scream in agony was the near red-hot metal above the wing-tanks and surrounding the engine cowling, fanned to glowing heat by the slipstream. After a time he forgot about his right hand and it became a tool, an extension of himself, a blistered mechanical implement as it grasped the exposed flaps of shot-up metal on the nacelles. He was even unaware of the smell of his own flesh burning as he worked the extinguisher nozzle into the area round the Merlin's cylinder block.

In the end, he realized it was not fear that he must overcome in himself, but pain. It was pain, not fear, that was sapping his strength and dizzily trying to force him into the holocaust at the trailing edge in order to ensure his destruction. After a time he saw that the flames were beginning to die away, but the pain in his right hand, and to a lesser degree his legs, remained.

When he was sure that there were no more flames sweeping back from the nacelle, he slid forward again to the leading edge, holding his right hand stiffly away from contact with the metal, but pressing the rest of his body as closely as he could to the wing, fearful of being flicked off by the slipstream, his left arm hooked round the leading edge as Fairclough pulled him in.

Inside the aircraft Hunting took in Collins' scorched battledress blouse and trousers at a glance, but he did not know the reason why Collins held his right hand behind his back.

Now, although the starboard inner Merlin juddered and rattled on its mounting, it was quite clear to all of them that the cracked fuel lead which had started the fire was no longer feeding it and all that was left were ebbing lines of flame across the carbon-blackened wing surface.

Fairclough said:

'I'd never have believed it in a thousand years. Talk about Jesus walking upon the water.'

Collins said:

'Someone had to go out there, but it turned out to be a piece of cake.' His face was white and strained in the dim cabin light.

He winced as the palm of his right hand came into contact with the metal of the fuselage.

'If you'll excuse me, I'll go back aft and put something on my hand. That wing was warm to the touch in places.'

Fairclough said:

'D'you want me to do it?'

'No, thanks awfully. I'll be all right. A dab of acriflavine and a piece of gauze will see me right in no time. Something to tide me over again until I can get to the quack.'

'O.K. Suit yourself.'

Collins lurched away from the pilot's compartment towards the rear fuselage.

'Right, Fairclough,' Hunting said. 'You better get busy and raise Darky, or we'll never make it on three engines and a busted altimeter.'

Fairclough said:

'Have you any idea where the hell we are?'

'Christ knows. According to the Professor, we should be halfway to the Isle of Wight by now. In any case they should fill you in on all that kind of gen. I'll switch on the IFF.'

'By the way, Cap,' Fairclough said, plugging in as he sat down at his table and switched on the receiver, 'I have finally lost the contact on the Monica. God knows what happened. Only Barton tried to get a shot in and he missed. It can only be another of life's unexplained mysteries.'

18

Darky

Halfway across to Beachy Head, Hunting found himself involved in another internal battle, and this time the enemy seemed more subtle and more difficult to overcome. The sergeant pilot now had the sensation that he was alone and that the rest of the crew had abandoned the plane, leaving him to look after Barton. Now he would fly on for ever at the controls of the wounded Lancaster in the same eternal limbo preceding the dawn.

The draught from the forward escape hatch increased this illusion as it whistled eerily over the dead control panel and past him to the empty rear turret. He even wished that someone's voice would come up over the intercom before he realized that this was all fantasy and it was affecting his judgement.

So strong was the feeling, however, that even when Fairclough eventually came up over the intercom to tell him that he had got through to Darky, Hunting could not be sure he had not imagined their conversation.

'Come up and tell me exactly what they said.'

'What's up, Cap?'

'Nothing. Just come round and tell me about it.'

'O.K. If that's what you want.'

Fairclough stood wondering what could have happened as Hunting sat silently hunched over the controls.

'They're giving us a course for Buckfield.'

'Where the hell's that?'

'Somewhere in Kent. Apparently they're laying on Sandra to guide us in. Even mentioned the QFE.'

Hunting gave a grim laugh.

'Very handy. Didn't you tell them our altimeter's u/s?'

'Yes, but they still insisted on telling me. When we cross the coast, they'll guide us in.'

Fairclough hesitated for a moment as if reluctant to go on.

'Feel like an orange, Cap?'

'Thanks, but you were going to tell me something else, weren't you?'

'That's right, Cap. I was. Apparently there are patches of ground fog.'

Hunting received this latest news without any visible sign of emotion, before going on to say:

'I don't know whether I can accept that risk on top of everything else, and we haven't enough height to jump. The cliffs around Beachy are getting on for six hundred. I think I ought to ditch.'

'What about Barton?'

Barton was, of course, the unresolved factor in the equation.

'To hell with it,' Hunting said bitterly. 'It looks as if we've used up all our luck this trip. And now I'm expected to ploughs onto some unknown field in the middle of Kent surrounded by hills and submerged in fog.'

Fairclough persisted, however.

'It would most likely be curtains for Barton if you were to ditch.'

Hunting said:

'So everyone keeps on telling me.'

'I'll switch you through on Darky, shall I, Cap?'

'O.K., but come back here when you've done it. Where's Maitland?'

'Keeping an eye on Barton.'

'What about Collins?'

'Somewhere aft of the main spar, seeing to his hands.'

'D'you think he's all right?'

'People like Collins are always all right, because he thinks he's some kind of a hero. Those types are natural survivors. He'll probably want you to put him in for a gong.'

'He'll be lucky. Well, anyway, I want him around too. So go and dig him out, will you? He can make himself useful at the controls while I have that orange.'

Hunting felt drained. A five-minute break could make all the difference with the tricky landing ahead. His arms now physically ached with effort as he rigidly kept the stick at the correct angle, his foot on the rudder to correct the Lancaster's tendency to edge to port now that the dead starboard inner had thrown the engines off balance. At the same time he strained at the panel, watching for the slightest dip in the revolution counters. It seemed to him that Fairclough was away for half an hour before he suddenly heard the crackle of sidetone through his head-set as the wireless operator connected him to the main receiver channel. Hunting looked up and saw that Collins was standing beside him, his right hand loosely covered with a black silk flying glove.

'O.K., Collins. Your dream has come true. I'm going to take time off to have this orange.'

'What do you mean by that, Cap?'

'Do I have to spell it out for you? You're going to take over and fly this bloody kite. Don't worry, it's quite simple. I've been doing it all night. All you've got to do is keep the nose up, use the rudder and keep your eyes firmly fixed on the rev counter.'

Collins stood beside him, apparently gripped with a strange rigid reluctance.

'You mean you want me to take over?'

'That's right. Just while I'm eating this orange. You were keen enough to do it before.'

Collins looked stonily out through the side window, his lip quivering.

'Don't ask me to do it, Cap. It's not possible.'

'What on earth do you mean, not possible? You were at Flying School, weren't you? Did a stint on Lancs? All I want is to be able to stand up for five minutes and have that orange. I shouldn't have thought that that was too much to ask.'

'I can't, Cap. I just can't. Don't ask me why.'

Hunting saw that tears were now silently trickling down the pilot officer's cheeks.

'Christ!' said Hunting bitterly. 'You windy or something? Don't you know I've got to take the bloody aircraft in through possible fog, onto an unknown airfield without any wheel brakes. D'you think I'm keen on that idea? I know you all want us to think that you're some kind of a hero, but just do me that one simple favour. Just give me a break. O.K.?'

Without another word and still staring out into the darkness, Collins stiffly raised his right hand and inch by painful inch removed the black silk glove, as though the least movement was agony.

Below the yellow of the acriflavine across his palm was a puffy mess of second-degree burns and pieces of flapping tissue. But below that, Hunting and Fairclough were both shocked to see claw-like ridges of bone running where the inside of his fingers should be.

'I can't, Cap. I just can't. I can hardly move it, let alone touch anything, let alone hold the bloody control column.'

Hunting said:

'O.K., O.K. I'm sorry, Collins, take it easy. I didn't know, did I?' Then he almost shouted, unable to erase the terrible memory of Collins' hand. 'For Christ's sake! Why did you have to keep that damn stiff upper lip? Why didn't you tell us in the first place? Then we'd have understood.'

Collins said:

'I know you may find this hard to believe, but I wanted to carry on as normal, that's all.'

'O.K. Well, you can't and you should have known better. You should be in the sick-bay. You should have done yourself a favour and not strained yourself so bloody hard. None of us are supermen, yourself included.'

Hunting regretted his outburst immediately, but nevertheless it made him feel slightly better. In any case it was true, whether the pilot officer liked it or not. By continuing his hero act, Collins had simply complicated the situation. As the pilot officer collapsed on the flight engineer's seat, Hunting could now see that Collins' burn injuries were not limited to his hands. The fabric of his scorched battledress had parted in many places, partially revealing the gigantic raw red blisters underneath.

'Have you taken anything to stop the pain?'

Collins shook his head.

'Fairclough, you better give him a morphia shot or something. The poor bugger must be in agony.'

'It's all right,' Collins said.

'It's bloody far from all right! Nobody's asking you to be a martyr.'

After a pause Fairclough said:

'O.K., Cap. I'll fix him up.'

Now that his secret had been revealed, Collins sat shivering in the cabin half-light, his previously wooden face contorted with pain.

Maitland had come back to the engineer's station when he found that he could get no response from Hunting over the intercom.

'Coast coming up, Cap. It looks like Newhaven. I picked out the visual beacon.'

'O.K.,' Hunting said grimly. 'I want you to stand by here, Professor. This landing is not going to be much fun for any of us.'

Fairclough gave Collins the morphia ampoule as Hunting switched on his mike.

'Hello, Darky Control. P Peter over.'

The WAAF's voice, cool and relaxed, came back to them distantly, as though from some other and scarcely remembered world.

'Hello, P Peter. This is Darky. We are tracking you. Turn on heading magnetic zero one fife for Buckfield at Beacon Mother Item. QFE one zero zero niner. Sandra is waiting.

Watching. Out.'

'Hello, Darky Control. This is P Peter. Wounded on board, and starboard inner failure means brakes u/s.'

'Hello, P Peter. This Darky. Roger.'

Then the channel became empty, crackling with sidetone.

'What the hell does she mean by "Roger" and then signing off?' Hunting said irritably.

Maitland said:

'Maybe she's gone to get another opinion. She sounded a right little cracker to me.'

'Come to that,' Hunting went on, 'I'm not exactly enthusiastic about the starboard undercart. In my view, the hydraulics may be all washed up.'

Then Hunting heard the WAAF's voice again:

'Hello, P Peter. This is Darky. Message received and understood. Talking you in. Landing turn priority. Look out for green. Watch for searchlight directional marker to port in three minutes. Avoid red flares on hills. Out.'

Maitland said:

'At least they seem to be concerned. Thank God the compass isn't u/s.'

Hunting said edgily:

'Tell me something that isn't.'

Maitland said:

'I see the SL.'

It seemed strange that a searchlight could be anything but hostile after what they had just been through.

The single finger of light wavered and then flicked quickly eastwards, returned, wavered and flicked over again. But Hunting saw that the beam at its base was soft and misty. The sidetone crackled in his earphones once more:

'Hello, P Peter. This is Darky Control. Corrected heading is magnetic zero one three. Your altitude is twelve fifty and falling.'

'Roger, Darky Control.'

Hunting altered the compass heading and then turned to Fairclough and Maitland.

'If I've got to bring this kite in, I want to do it properly. Maitland, you can call the checks.'

'O.K., Cap.' Maitland said reluctantly.

The heavy bomber throbbed on through the darkness, losing height imperceptibly.

'And Fairclough, just keep your eyes peeled for Sandra.'

'Sandra shows the way,' Fairclough said and they all laughed, except for Collins. Sandra was usually depicted as a girl delicately raising her skirt to reveal stocking tops and suspenders.

'Good old Sandra.'

Maitland wondered who had dreamed that name up for a flare-path.

'Come on, Professor, stop arsing about and extract your ruddy digit.'

'The trouble is I don't see much point.'

'Then I'll tell you the point,' Hunting said patiently. 'We're in trouble enough as it is, but the pre-landing check will tell me what is and what isn't working, O.K.?'

'None of it's working. It's a flying junk heap.'

Maitland was amazed that an aircraft could stay in the air for so long with so much going against it.

'The trouble with you, Maitland, is that you're a ruddy perfectionist. So far as you're concerned, if the paintwork's scratched the car won't start.'

Maitland looked puzzled for a moment and then shrugged.

'Anyway, we're wasting time,' Hunting said. 'Just get on with the check.'

'Auto-pilot control cock.'

'Out.'

'Superchargers.'

'Low ratio.'

'Air intake.'

'Cold.'

'Brake pressure.'

There was an uneasy pause as Hunting said angrily:

'Should supply 250-300 lb pressure. But is u/s.'

Fairclough said:

'There goes Sandra. The lady with the lamp.'

The night ahead of them was lit up by the two parallel

lines of flare-path lights that had suddenly been switched on ahead of them.

Hunting said:

'Anyway, Professor, it's impossible to increase to the recommended speed. 130 mph will have to do, and I aim to hit the deck at very much less than that without any wheel brakes.'

'Flaps.'

There was another anxious pause as Hunting shifted the selector lever, watching the hand on the Flaps Indicator Dial.

'Working.'

Hunting quickly moved the selector back, frightened in case he should disturb the carefully poised attitude of the aircraft, to say nothing of the risks involved in reducing air-speed.

'Undercarriage.'

Again they bent over the instrument, waiting for the red lights to change as Hunting opened the inner starboard throttle and moved the selector lever. Then he said:

'I have green, for what that's worth. Fairclough, you better go forward and check.'

They felt the inner starboard engine shudder gently on the wing as the undercarriage dropped down into position.

'Propeller.'

'2,400 rpm. That's the best I can do.'

Hunting eased the stick forward as wisps of fog suddenly dimmed the flare-path.

'O.K. I'll try this time round. But I can see damn all.'

For an instant, Maitland caught sight of the Watch Office with the ambulance and fire tender crawling off the tarmac onto the perimeter track to meet them.

'Flaps.'

Hunting said through his teeth:

'Down.' As they heard the whistle of compressed air, the Lancaster began to nudge down towards the first pair of flare-path lights at the steep angle induced by the flaps.

'Fuel.'

'Booster pumps on in tanks in use.'

Fairclough had, by this time, made his way back from the forward gun-turret.

'They're down,' he said. 'But whether the starboard undercart's properly locked the way the whole nacelle is screwing about, is anyone's guess.'

'The panel light says it's O.K.'

But even as Hunting spoke, the green lights confirming that the undercarriage was locked down flickered on and off once and then went out.

Hunting felt his head spin in a sudden surge of panic. They must be almost at the start of the runway at no more than fifty feet.

'There goes the green,' Maitland said.

Over the receiver circuit Hunting heard the voice of the Darky WAAF once more:

'Hello, P Peter. This is Darky Control. You are on course and should have a visual of the runway. Pancake. Pancake.'

At that moment the Lancaster's nose crept into a low-lying fogbank that drifted like a curtain in front of the flare-path, reducing the lights to a distant and uncertain glimmer. Hunting instinctively pulled back at the stick and the Lancaster hovered for a moment as the engines attempted to climb with the flaps down. The Lancaster's nose began to rise.

'Jesus Christ!' said Fairclough. 'Don't drop a wing at this stage. In any case, I wish you wouldn't do things like that.'

'It's only because I can see damn all.'

'The bloody cure's worse than the disease.'

The three straining engines were not, however, able to maintain the climbing attitude and the Lancaster gradually slid back, and the nose too began to fall.

'We're going to bloody prang, I know it,' Maitland said between his teeth.

As soon as he sensed the downward movement, the sergeant pilot desperately increased throttle and moved the flap selector forward.

'Shut up! Shut up!' Hunting shouted.

'Hello, P Peter. This is Darky Control ...'

But then there was a sudden silence and a loud crash from the rear of the aircraft as the tail wheel smashed onto the tarmac, while the nose of the Lancaster hovered momentarily twenty feet above the ground. Then it dropped as the aircraft travelled forward at a velocity of ninety miles an hour, and the undercarriage struck the tarmac with a heavy thud.

For a second they held a normal attitude, although the tail wheel had been ripped off and the rear fuselage was dragged screaming along the runway surface with a stream of sparks spurting from either side of the castor mounting. Then, with a second unnerving crash, the starboard oleo undercarriage struts buckled and collapsed at the same time that Hunting switched off the engines and the master fuel cock.

The aircraft now swung off the flare-path in a wild arc, pivoting on the starboard wing nacelles as the propellers bent back and scythed into the damp dew-bound earth and the standing crops that lined the runway, until the Lancaster had revolved to half-face the approach.

The crew had been thrown against the starboard fuselage in a wild confusion of oxygen bottles, cable leads and other flotsam by this abrupt application of centrifugal force. Collins lay moaning on the floor as Hunting unstrapped his safety harness and pulled himself out of his seat, already only too well aware of the pungent and all-pervading smell of petrol vapour.

'Abandon! Get out! Get out!'

Maitland hobbled to his feet, nursing a cracked wrist, and pushed himself through the opening that Collins had cut in the fuselage beside the flight engineer's panel what seemed to be hours ago.

Fairclough paused:

'What about Barton, Cap?'

'I'll get Barton out. Just you see to Collins.'

Hunting felt stiff and unsteady on his feet after the time he had spent at the controls. As he stumbled back, he barked his shins as he climbed into the rest bay, where Barton was sitting and shaking his head.

'What the hell's happening to this aircraft?'

'Christ, don't you know? We pranged on landing. The petrol could go up any minute.'

Barton smiled and said:

'There can't be much left of that.'

Then he nodded to the rear fuselage:

'But it doesn't look as though we'll need to use the front door.'

The oval of the fuselage abruptly ended at a point where the tail plane and rear turret had broken away from the main fuselage aft of the upper turret.

'I'm glad I wasn't looking for Nightfighters when all that happened.'

Hunting said:

'For Christ's sake, there's no time to frig about.' Through the window he could see asbestos-suited firemen running out the hoses from the tender.

Hunting hardly glanced at the motionless body of McIndoe as he pulled Barton back down the fuselage. Then Barton said:

'Don't worry, Cap. You got us down and out of trouble. Take my word for it. I wouldn't fly with any other crew.'

19

Interrogation

Four of P for Peter's crew were at interrogation. The squadron-leader who was on duty did not seem particularly pleased to see them. He wore a greying toothbrush moustache and the 1914-15 Star.

There should have been only three of them, but when the truck had taken them back to the Ops Room from the shattered remains of their Lancaster, Collins had found a new lease of life. The morphia he had taken was beginning to wear off, so that he was able to make his own decisions against a deadened background of pain. The pilot officer had politely but firmly insisted that he should attend the de-briefing, since he wanted to hear how the raid had gone.

The other three were not quite sure whether this was not just an excuse for another display of line-shooting and kept on exchanging uneasy glances as they sat round the wooden table, drinking mugs of rum-laced tea. In spite of this, Hunting could not remember tasting anything quite as good in all his life.

The lights were low in the Ops Room. The squadron-leader soon exhausted the military aspects of the raid, taking notes about the Nightfighter tactics and the flak and search-light positions that Maitland had pinpointed. He was clearly anxious to return to the comfort of his bed as soon as possible and went straight on to the only other outstanding points.

'And where's the missing crew member, Sergeant?'

'You mean Howells, the Flight Engineer?'

'That's right, the Flight Engineer. There's a dead Air Gunner. We know all about him, but what happened to the missing Flight Engineer?'

Hunting hesitated.

'Sergeant McIndoe was shot up by flak.'

'Yes, yes. I know all about Sergeant McIndoe. I'm quite clear in my mind about him. It's the other fellow I want to hear about.'

'I'm not quite sure what happened to Sergeant Howells, sir.'

The squadron-leader put down his silver propelling pencil with a gesture of irritation.

'Bloody hell, Sergeant! What d'you mean, "Not quite sure"?'

'What I mean is,' Hunting continued as patiently as he could, 'that I wasn't there when it happened. I ordered Sergeant Howells forward to the air bomber's compartment to assist Pilot Officer Collins to clear a jam in the bomb release mechanism.'

The squadron-leader looked at Collins while Hunting, Fairclough and Maitland waited for the pilot officer's blow-by-blow account of what had really happened before pinning the putty medal for 'Lack of Moral Fibre' well and truly on Howells' absent chest.

The last thing that Hunting wanted was any post mortem involving cowardice. P for Peter's crew contained the nucleus for a team now, and anything like the incident in the air bomber's compartment should be kept within the family. He could only hope that Collins would sense this. It was something that no one could tell him.

Collins said:

'It's very simple really. Our cookie hung up and Sergeant Howells tried to get to the bomb-bay to deal with the fault. However, he was out of luck and was swept through the forward hatch, though fortunately he had his chute.'

'It sounds crazy to me. Why didn't you try and stop him? In any case, the only bomber that gives you access to the bomb-bay that I'm aware of is the Fortress.'

'Well, he reckoned he could do it. The slip gear had jammed. He was quite determined to go.'

The squadron-leader said:

'The clot. Now I've heard everything.'

'Are you doubting my word, sir?'

'Of course not, not at all.'

He pencilled something on his pad.

'I'll put him down as missing, but no doubt Group may be interested. You'll draw it to the attention of your own CO, I expect?'

'Absolutely.'

The squadron-leader stared into Collins' tired young face.

'Well, sounds as if you've had your fair share of thrills and spills. Flak, Messerschmitts. Seems like you put up a pretty good show.'

'We all worked together as a team, but it was Sergeant Pilot Hunting that took us there and got us back.'

'Yes, of course, I'd forgotten about that. Oh yes, one other thing. Your starboard inner burned up. What happened there?'

He looked over to Hunting again.

'The Pilot Officer used his initiative.'

'Tell me about it, Sergeant. You're not saying he went wing-walking or anything? Two candidates for a decoration would be too much on your first op.'

They waited as Hunting lit another Players and slowly inhaled. Then Collins interrupted again:

'Oh no, sir. I'm not that kind of a hero. I just try and do my job.'

'Very commendable,' said the squadron-leader. 'Then I can take it, it was you that put out the fire?'

'I used the extinguisher, but it blew itself out when the fuel from number 3 tank was jettisoned.'

'Just like that?'

'Just like that, sir.'

'I see. Well, that seems to cover everything. You'll be credited with a probable for the first Nightfighter. That is, unless there's confirmation from any other bomber that happened to be in the area at the time. We'll send on the photoflash pictures for your ladder if we can find the camera. It sounds like a very good night's work, Collins. Well done!'

Hunting was conscious of another crew waiting restlessly for their turn in the queue behind them near the doorway.

'Can we get through to Clixby Wolds, sir?'

'Help yourself. There's a coinbox in the hall outside.'

'You haven't such a thing as a sixpence or a shilling, by any chance?'

'I don't believe I have. You'll get your railway warrants in the morning. Your aircraft is a write-off as you may imagine. You can bed down for the night in one of the Nissens. The Orderly Sergeant will show you where.'

The squadron-leader shuffled his pad to indicate that the interrogation was over so far as he was concerned.

'Thanks awfully,' Collins said.

After they had left the Ops Room, Fairclough said:

'What do they call this place? Bullshit Castle? He'll be inviting us to dig our own graves next. Christ, what wouldn't I do for a drink!'

Hunting glanced at Collins:

'We'd have to try the Sergeants' Mess for that.'

'If you sign me in, I'd like to buy you all a round before I report to the MI Room.'

'O.K. You're on,' said Hunting.

The Sergeants' Mess was open after hours that night because of the pressure from other bomber crews who had been diverted to Buckfield.

The Halifax crew of *Melancholy Baby*, had arrived back with exhausted fuel tanks, a smashed compass and an incendiary container hung up in the bomb-bay. Now full of the euphoria brought on by their survival, they were gathered round the piano celebrating. The tune was *The Church's One Foundation*, but the words were quite different.

'We are the heavy bombers, we fly through endless shit.
Flak-bursts and concentrations and occasionally we're hit.
So when we drop our bollocks, we do not give a damn.
The eggs may miss the goods yard, but they fuck up
  poor old Hamm.'

The atmosphere was thick with cigarette smoke and echoed with nervous excited laughter as the air-crews relived the highlights of the operation.

Collins ordered four pints and said:

'I hope my performance went down all right.'

Hunting said:

'I couldn't have done better myself, and it certainly seemed to impress our RFC veteran.'

'And when the weather's shitty and winds are all to hell,
The navigator's balled-up, the R/T's balled as well.
We think of all the popsies we've laid in days gone by,
And curse the stupid bastards who taught us how to fly.'

Fairclough said:

'Yes, we owe you a great deal, sir, with your fire brigade

act. Cheers. Up the Führer!'

They all laughed at that.

Collins said:

'We all owe each other a great deal. Tonight's been pretty revealing so far as I'm concerned. I hope I'll be flying again with you blokes soon.'

'And in the Heavenly Ops Room, St Peter will enquire:
Did you just drop a cookie? Or start a damn great fire?
But when you see the angels, tapping their faultless morse,
You'll know then that your QDM was a reciprocal course.'

Maitland said:

'That certainly goes for me too. But hadn't you better go and get fixed up at the MI Room?'

'I should, but I'd rather be here, Professor. By the way, how's Barton?'

'O.K., I think. Chiefly a broken arm from what I could make out. They'll patch him up in no time at all. Pity about that kite.'

'It was a good kite. It deserved a better fate.'

Fairclough said:

'It was a ropey kite. Just think of all that engine trouble.'

'O.K. It was a ropey kite. But I still think we ought to buy it on the never-never to put on the mantelpiece.'

They all laughed again at that.

Collins said:

'Will you take my guns back?'

Hunting said:

'We'll bring back all the guns. If necessary, we'll send them luggage in advance by LNER if we can't get a taxi to King's Cross.'

'And if you go to Hades, it's just like SHQ.
There's lots of stooges sitting with fuck all else to do.
When they ask you for your flimsies, your target maps and pass,
Then take the ruddy issue and shove it up their arse.'

There was an outburst of cheering with air-crew miming rude V-signs, blowing raspberries and pretending to pull lavatory chains.

Fairclough said:

'It must have gone well. There can't be that many losses.'

Hunting said:

'It was a good operation and P for Peter came out on top. In fact, we all did.'

'Well,' said Collins, 'I'd better be getting along now and find out what it's like to be a guinea pig.'

Hunting said:

'Don't forget to drop us a postcard.'

'You'll pass on the general form to Barton's popsie?'

'You mean the chop girl? Of course I will.'

They all laughed again and then Hunting said:

'I tried to get through to Clixby, but there's an hour's delay. Jerry's been having a go at London again and all the lines are down or busy.'

Collins hesitated for a moment and then said:

'I'm sorry about the cock-up.'

Hunting said:

'We all make cock-ups from time to time. Nobody's perfect. It only gets serious when someone doesn't extract their finger so it isn't sorted out.'

A few minutes later, Collins said 'Goodbye' and went out into the blackout in search of the Duty MO. Although the others wanted to go along with him to see that he was all right, he refused the offer.

'Nobody's going to blame me for breaking up the party.'

'Nobody's blaming you for anything.'

After he had gone, they were silent until Fairclough bought them all another round, as they individually went over the common experience of the last seven hours.

Fairclough said:

'That gussie's a funny kind of hero. He grows on you.'

Hunting said:

'He may be a line-shooter, but it's all a great big front. Deep down he's all right. He certainly sorted out that uniformed bureaucrat at the de-briefing.'

Maitland said:

'Anyway, let's drink to the silly bugger. Let's drink to all of us, come to that, including McIndoe. And not forgetting Howells, the poor misguided sod.'

20

The Morning After the Night Before

The next morning, Hunting, Fairclough and Maitland, with three parachutes, four valises and eight Brownings, caught the 6.50 from Tunbridge Wells, so that an hour and a half later they were in Waterloo.

It took them a further one and a half hours to travel the two and a quarter miles north across the Thames to King's Cross because they could not get a cab and the tube was closed.

The ten o'clock train for Edinburgh (Waverley) had been delayed half an hour, but since they were on duty, they were able to by-pass the queue which stretched from Platform One out and through the adjacent ruins in York Way.

There were no cigarettes for sale, although Maitland was able to buy that week's copy of the 'Picture Post'.

Hunting, Fairclough and Maitland stood in the narrow corridor of the LNER Third Class coach next to the guard's van to keep an eye on the kit, particularly the guns. The corridor smelled stale, and the blinds were down in most of the brown teak-panelled compartments; the corridor windows had been painted a transparent blue against the blackout. In any case, there were no seats. Every inch of the train was packed with standing servicemen together with their kit-bags, packs, arms and attaché cases: infantry returning from leave to their units in the North of England, bereted Signals and Armoured Corps to Yorkshire and Commandos to the 'Protected Area' beyond Inverness; together with Naval ratings and Petty Officers on their way to Scapa by way of Thurso.

After the train had pulled out of the station, they spent the next hour crawling out along an improvised loop-line at the Caledonian Road, playing brag and pontoon with the dog-eared card pack Fairclough had produced. The main line north out of London was still being repaired after the previous night's bombing.

Then the train gathered speed through the northern suburbs, passing RAF Stanmore and row upon row of recently built semi-detached houses. The Anderson shelters in their back gardens were occasionally obscured by drifting streams of engine smoke. Sometimes, when they passed a hoarding, they would read: 'KEEP AT IT' *and* 'LEND TO DEFEND THE RIGHT TO BE FREE.'

At last they left the barrage balloons, wardens' posts, static water-tanks ack-ack emplacements behind, crossing the sunny fields of Hertfordshire and the Welwyn Viaduct into the deceptive peace of the soft rolling English countryside.

From time to time the railway line ran parallel with the A1 North, where they overtook or crossed the convoys crawling south and north: Gunner regiments with Quads, limbers and twenty-five pounders; three-tonners packed with shirtless and leather-belted infantry; or solitary RAF Queen Marys carrying Lancaster or Spitfire sections.

Before Peterborough, the land opened out with a flat echo of the Fens in wide, interminable fields, where scarf-covered women and Polish farmworkers stooped and knelt over the late potato harvest, with a shire-horse and wagon standing patiently in the distance behind them.

They got off at Doncaster at two o'clock and took a trolley for their equipment, before giving up their warrants to the woman ticket-collector in slacks and flashing their Movement Order at the Air Police staff-sergeants in their white webbing at the barrier.

Hunting said:

'We'll scrub round the RTO. They could keep us hanging about all day. I'll book a taxi.'

Even the capacious boot of the pre-war Morris could scarcely hold all their equipment.

As he turned off the Great North Road to take the A18 for Scunthorpe, the taxi-driver broke his silence:

'Been on an op, lads?'

Mindful of security, Hunting said:

'Something like that.'

'Too bad you couldn't bring back your kite. They said they cost £20,000 to build at the last "Wings for Victory". Mind you, the money's very good in the factories. I've a sister-in-law that was directed to Littlewood's. She had to go, but she makes a bomb at it, overtime and all. Lanc fuselages and Hallibasher floors mostly.'

'We got most of ours back,' Hunting said. 'I expect that bits of it will fly again.'

'They said it was Emsdorf on the eight o'clock news. Seventeen copped it. You must be one of the lucky ones.'

'Then it sounds like a good raid.'

'I'd be in there myself with you. Always respect the boys in blue, but I'd never get through the medical. Straight C3. As well as that, I wear glasses.'

Fairclough said:

'Sergeant Maitland wears them too. You look O.K. to me.'

'Well, there's this suspected blood condition, makes me tire easily. I'm having tests at the cottage hospital, but the specialists can't quite put their finger on it. And then there's Brenda's nerves. She could never manage with me away from home. Anyway, this racket's almost a reserved occupation, ferrying you bods between the Groups and Doncaster. The money's only fair, but it's the only way I can lay my hands on the pool petrol.'

None of them felt like saying much. When they passed through Bigby, they knew they were almost there.

'Mind you, I've got a brother who's Merchant Navy. Been torpedoed twice. One time he was three days off Lisbon on a Carling float. He's either born lucky or off his rocker. Depends how you look at it.'

Fairclough said:

'I suppose it does. It certainly takes all sorts.'

At the main gate at Clixby Wolds, the wind was sighing through the telephone lines as they returned the eight Brownings to the armoury and handed in their parachutes to the WAAF corporal at Stores.

She told them that six aircraft were on strength after the raid, of which five were operational. O for Oboe had not returned, while P for Peter at Buckfield made up the negative balance. Hunting nervously tried to work out a logic in this alphabet relationship, rather like a punter evaluating a roulette system. He reached no positive conclusions, but it seemed as rational a way of looking at it as any.

McIndoe's room had already been sealed, so Hunting left his effects with the Padre.

'He was a brave boy. It's a bad show.'

Hunting had the feeling that this was the Padre's standard comment on dead air-crew. He couldn't blame him for saying it. He had, after all, to say something, and what else could he say? He remembered the immobile bloodstained corpse under the parachute canopy in front of the flare-chute. McIndoe hadn't looked horrific or disgusting. He was just a nothing. At least they hadn't had to hose out the pieces, but could remove him decently on a stretcher.

'A very bad show.'

With a jolt Hunting realized that he could remember very little about the Canadian except his obsession for escape.

He left the quarters quickly, finding it too depressing a reminder of the possible outcome for them all, and started to make his way over to the mess.

On the way he found Fairclough and Maitland standing at the notice board, examining the Battle Order.

'We're on again tonight,' Maitland said in disbelief, hardly able to credit what he had read. 'There must have been some balls-up. Barton's name's there too.'

Hunting read the three other meaningless names that

had been assigned to his crew:

'No more bloody officers. At least that's something.'

Fairclough said:

'A.G. Sergeant Grimond, F.E. Sergeant Minshell and Sergeant Cox, Air Bomber. You'd have thought they'd have given us a break.'

'Why the hell should they? There's a war on, isn't there? We're not flying scheduled flights for BOAC.'

'They must be keen to see us finish our tour.'

'The Ruhr battle's a maximum effort job, all of us know that. We knew what to expect when we signed on. At least, I did. So far as Barton's concerned, A.G.s are like gold-dust in the Command. I even heard they've been putting out a call to the ruddy Army to fill the gaps. That's why Barton's back on call.'

Maitland said:

'For Christ's sake, Barton was in a bad way, blood all over the place.'

'You know bugger all about it, Professor. The medics must have classified it as "upper limb soft tissues", not even a fracture. They probably only had to slap on some iodine and an Elastoplast to keep out the dirt.'

They found the Australian sitting at the bar wearing a new dark-blue battledress top. It was impossible to tell that he had been wounded.

Hunting said:

'They didn't hang about discharging you.'

'Too bloody true. I got sent back last night on a Signals truck. Ten stitches across my biceps and that was it. My arm's a bit stiff, but I reckon I can still drink my ale left-handed and press the tit on the Brownings. What else is there for me to do in life? Did you bring back the guns?'

Fairclough said:

'Maitland here seemed to think you were on the danger list. I'm glad he's wrong, but they might have given you a 72-hour pass for services rendered.'

'What? Look in on the Nightfighters round Piccadilly Circus? No, I'll be fixed up much better here at Clixby.'

'Oh, you mean Sergeant Nicholls?'

'She comes off watch in half an hour. Anyway, not to worry, Cap. We've got K for King this time.'

'Any kind of form?'

'Twenty-six ops without too much trouble. The crew's been posted to Coastal.'

'Quite an old lady.'

'The Chiefie gave her a big build-up, said the engines ran like a bitch on heat.'

Hunting said:

'Let's hope he's right.'

'She's been flight-tested. Minshell, the new F.E., reckons she's a runner.'

'Let's hope he's right too.'

Already the sergeant pilot was trying to assess the new situation. It would be time for briefing again soon.

'What's the new crew like?'

'Minshell arrived yesterday. Grimond's from another crew, a loner. They've just had their original A.G. rejoin. I don't know much about Cox, but they all seem O.K. Grimond's a tough cookie and he's chalked up over fifteen ops. He seems to think he knows it all. I got the feeling he wasn't too keen to go with us, but he didn't have any choice.'

'I'd like to know who does. If he was that hot, he should have been picked up by a master bomber or the Pathfinders.'

'That's what he seems to be hoping for.'

Hunting said:

'What's the buzz about possible targets?'

'Hamburg or gardening off Heligoland – the fuel load's right for either.'

'Let's hope to God it's Heligoland. Hamburg's a pretty hot number.'

Maitland said:

'You can say that again.'

There was a roar overhead as a Lancaster on test-flight rattled the glasses on the bar as it came in low for the final approach.

Already Hunting was beginning to put to one side the details of last night's raid on Emsdorf. There were new factors now, new considerations that would affect all of them. He said to Maitland:

'You better pick up as much gen as you can on the Hamburg flak, unofficially, of course.'

'I share your view.'

As Maitland turned away, refusing Barton's offer of a drink, Hunting could see three sergeants standing at the doorway.

Barton said:

'Those are our boys.'

When they came over as the Australian waved with a wince, Hunting tried to read their faces and get their measure. There would be little enough time before tonight to find out what made them tick.

But then there was never enough time for anything in this war, whether it involved a decision to take evasive action, heave a full bomb-load off the deck, or give the order to abandon. There was only enough time once the wrong decision had been made and everyone was dead. Hunting only intended to kill the enemy.

As the sergeants introduced themselves, Hunting only half listened, looking out through the window as he had done the day before to the predatory dark silhouettes of the Lancasters standing waiting at Dispersals.

He glanced at the clouds. The base of the cumulus must be lying at ten thousand feet and it was broken in patches, maybe four-tenths. Tonight they would all of them be above that cloud that stretched eastwards, across the North Sea to Germany. Tomorrow he would really get his head down and get in some sleep.

A selection of Bestsellers from Mayflower Books

Novels

EMMANUELLE	Emmanuelle Arsan	60p	☐
THE FURTHER EXPERIENCES OF EMMANUELLE	Emmanuelle Arsan	80p	☐
OIL	Jonathan Black	75p	☐
THE WORLD RAPERS	Jonathan Black	75p	☐
THE FOOTBALLER	Derek Dougan	75p	☐
PIPER'S LEAVE	Alexander Fullerton	60p	☐
OTHER MEN'S WIVES	Alexander Fullerton	50p	☐
BURY THE PAST	Alexander Fullerton	50p	☐
THE ESCAPISTS	Alexander Fullerton	50p	☐
THE PUBLISHER	Alexander Fullerton	50p	☐
STORE	Alexander Fullerton	40p	☐
CHIEF EXECUTIVE	Alexander Fullerton	40p	☐
I, A SAILOR	Morgen Holm	60p	☐
I, A PROSTITUTE	Nina Holm	35p	☐
I, A WOMAN	Siv Holm	35p	☐
I, SUSANNE	Susanne Holm	40p	☐
I, A TEENAGER	Tine Holm	40p	☐
KOPTIC COURT	Herbert Kastle	75p	☐
THE WORLD THEY WANTED	Herbert Kastle	75p	☐
LITTLE LOVE	Herbert Kastle	50p	☐
MIAMI GOLDEN BOY	Herbert Kastle	60p	☐
THE MOVIE MAKER	Herbert Kastle	95p	☐
THE STORY OF SAN MICHELE	Axel Munthe	75p	☐
AMANDA IN SPAIN	George Revelli	50p	☐
AMANDA'S CASTLE	George Revelli	35p	☐
RESORT TO WAR	George Revelli	35p	☐
COMMANDER AMANDA NIGHTINGALE	George Revelli	35p	☐
DOCTOR, NO!	William Rice	50p	☐
DOCTOR, DON'T!	William Rice	50p	☐
AN INTERRUPTED FRIENDSHIP	E. L. Voynich	50p	☐
THE GADFLY	E. L. Voynich	40p	☐
THE COAST OF FEAR	Leslie Waller	60p	☐
NUMBER ONE	Leslie Waller	60p	☐
A CHANGE IN THE WIND	Leslie Waller	40p	☐
THE AMERICAN	Leslie Waller	60p	☐